Rules for Dating a Demon

Amanda Humes

Copyright © 2023 by Amanda Humes

ISBN: 979-8-9886690-0-5 (Paperback)
       979-8-9886690-1-2 (Ebook)

Olympus Story House

Contents

Dedication

To everyone that has supported me in the journey that is life. To my mom, for buying me romance novels when I was young. To my dad who is no longer with us I wish you were here to see this. To my sister who wanted me to write and to my American Public University Class that made this book possible.

Glossary

Get – (n) a child of a demon.

Hubris – Greek for excessive pride.

Unacknowledged get – (n) usually a slur on par with human bastard. A demon child that father has not acknowledged.

Chapter 1

Len watched covertly the lovely creature that had stolen his imagination since he saw her as a young boy. Her ebony hair fell in inky black waves he wanted to get lost in. He should not be spying, or prying but he wanted to know more about the red skinned Meg.

Len already knew she was part demon and still he wanted her. Though he doubted he would ever find the courage to approach her. Not even in a city as large as New York, where Meg just happened to stand out to him.

******

Meg went about her normal life even though she felt something was going to happen. It was time to stock up on supplies and be by herself. She knew that it was getting to be breeding time. Meg had one friend, Griff, who joked about having some feelings for her. The demon under lord was sculpted like a Greek god. Yet he had never made a move on her and Meg had never really thought of him like that. Griff's face was a little gruff. The demon showed more on the outside on him than it did in her.

He had always seemed to be there for her since about the time she was old enough to know the stigma against her. Even in the demon world there were stigmas to be had, the worst being the unacknowledged get. Meg's father had never claimed his parental right, or at least take the spoils of knowing he had one upped a mortal. So, she was the dreaded unacknowledged get.

She like most female demon spawn was a sex demon. Though unlike most of Meg's kind she only indulged in the pleasures of the flesh when she knew she wouldn't carry a baby. Meg refused to have another soulless one aboard the planet.

Perhaps it was because of a lack of knowledge of her father just scarred her for that part of life. It was a matter of pride with her that she had been true to herself. In fact, Meg had been true to herself for hundreds of years.

Then all went black on Meg.

Chapter 2

It was a cheap motel room that smelled of bizarrely candy.

Meg thought as she started to come to. The yellowed paper was peeling off the walls. She sat on a lumpy bed. Then she saw the large cherub like body and groaned. The candy smell was that of an angel. Meg held back her curses as only an elder demon can.

Meanwhile Len jumped when Meg awoke. He had been secreted to this room as well. He wanted to offer for her comfort, yet more basic needs jumped to the forefront. Though Meg had the headache from Hades, she knew someone had set her up. She looked at Len from beneath her long lashes and knew he was not the mastermind of this. He was way too young. He had short sandy blonde hair and an adorably chubby body. Len was too innocent.

She realized where her thoughts and feelings were going and she shot from the sagging bed. She ran to the door, even though her poor brain knew she was locked in. Even, Meg, in panic strength couldn't get the door to budge.

She felt a soft yet strong hand at her back. Meg turned toward Len. The angel was taller than her and a quick visual assessment of their size differences made it more real. A shiver went through her as she realized he could break her petite frame. That just made her feel all the smaller, "We are trapped."

Meg felt flushed when his face didn't reflect any disgust. A pure angel would be fighting the feelings. Unfortunately, for her he must be a half breed. Before she realized it, he was kissing a tear that trailed down her face, "You do not have to be scarred."

"You don't—"he kissed her and it didn't feel like the kiss of an innocent or that of the disgusted.

"We shouldn't," was her final word of protest.

*****

Again, Meg awoke with an aching head, making her wonder if she hadn't been drugged. All her brain cells tried to figure out who would do this. She had no idea. Maybe she was not being targeted for anything but shook the thought away. Meg remembered how tough the door was to open. Angels did not do things like this; play jokes this serious among themselves.

She carefully put on the clothing that was tattered by big hands, luckily the owner was still asleep. One thing Meg was never good at was the morning after. She liked her relations one night and slide away like a beautiful figment of the other person's imagination. Meg went to the door and it opened with an ease that took her aback. She followed the cracked paper to the front desk. There she attempted to get information from the man at the desk. Though the man was totally enamored with her, but he could only tell her the room was paid for in cash.

Cash? No one used cash everything was done with plastic. The clerk even showed her the pay stub. Someone that didn't want to be known had set her up to corrupt that poor angel boy. Meg could only be thankful that the angel didn't have wings. That would be a sin beyond which she could live. Not that she didn't think something monumental might have happened to link them forever. She could only hope her timing was off.

*****

Len uncurled from the shabby accommodations. He wasn't surprised Meg was gone like a dream. Though in his deepest hopes he had hope she would stay with him. Then he looked at the ruined wallpaper, felt the lumpy bed and realized this wasn't the love nest that he would have wanted. Though the room was a colossal disaster he would remember this night for all his days.

Meg had been wild and uninhibited after a while. The girl certainly wasn't a shy one. She had full body participated. They'd done things he hadn't known were possible. It could only lead him to believe that maybe they were not as beyond one another's reach after all.

*****

Len could no longer help himself. That lovely night had been three months ago. He would have called her if he had her number. Though knowing her, Meg probably didn't have a phone. Yet he knew where she lived, he'd followed her one night by foot. It was time to talk. Len wasn't one to do a one night stand, especially not with Meg.

His skin did crawl as he went to the smoky alley, she lived in. It smelled of fire and of brimstone. The chimney must not just be for show because smoke was coming out of it. Puffing away like a smoker promising his last cigarette.

On the outside it really was a homely house. It was old yet well loved. The brick and mortar was easy to see in construction. It wasn't like the others; it had the enchantment that only the angels and demons could make. Before he could knock, she pulled him inside. He felt an unexpected punch to his gut as he noticed that she had a paleness in her red skin.

"What—" both started.

"What are you doing here!" Meg exclaimed as she bustled around to close all the curtains, "Does anyone know you are here?"

"I thought it was time we talked," Len proclaimed.

Her eyes changed from dark to an unholy shade of fire, "Talk?!" Then her eyes faded back to their regular shade and she hurried to her bathroom. Len was startled but he followed her as she just made it to the bathroom to empty the contents of her stomach. With the grace of a princess she pulled her hair from her face as she got up, "I'm afraid I'm not in the mood to chat."

Len softened, "You're sick. Why don't I help you mend and then when you feel like speaking—"

"Help me mend!" she thundered, "Are you serious?" again there was a warning sparkle to her eyes. Him sticking around was the last thing she needed around.

"You're too proud," Len concluded, "I want to help you." "You've helped me enough," she growled.

Len threw himself on the couch, "Are you this rude to everyone that—"he stopped himself. He did the math and took in her paleness. "Holy Lu! You're pregnant."

"Watch your tongue," Meg snapped," the last thing we need is you calling the attention of Hades on us."

Len got up, "But you are pregnant?"

"Of course I am," She wanted to sucker punch him. Though it wouldn't do any good the deed was done. In a hotel that rented by the hour no less.

Len being young said, "That's great."

"Are you insane?" she truly wondered as he got happier, "If you have forgotten the small details that I'm a demon and you are an angel."

"I'm half an angel."

Meg nodded, "I thought as much."

Now was Len's turn to get angry, "What does that mean anyway?"

"You are too young to know the rules in the war between Heaven and Hell."

He drew up to his full height, "I know enough to know my side should be upset and your side should be happy."

The truth was more powerful than a slap. She should be happy that she'd outsmarted an angel, "You wouldn't understand," she dismissed, "How can someone that grew up with a loving mother could?"

He wouldn't protest though it was his aunt that had raised him. He felt a little guilt not telling her the whole truth. But he had his own secrets. Things he didn't let anyone know.

"I was raised as a foundling." That made him blanch, "Mother didn't have a choice. It was throw me out. Or they got rid of us both." That she had been born on a ship she omitted. Though they shared a child now didn't mean he need all her secrets. That included her few memories after her birth nor her estimated age. "Will you keep it?" he sobered.

She expelled a humorless laugh, "Even among demons children are sacred. More prized than some mortals make them. I'll have the baby but if it turns out like you, the child could be a pawn. More so if it has the blood of all three. There is a small chance that it will be born a mere mortal."

He looked down at his feet before looking her in the eye and asking, "Were you going to tell me?"

Angry at the situation she yelled, "How can I tell someone I don't know?"

Shamed he responded, "That is a terrible excuse, Meg." She flinched, "How do you know my name?"

"You said it that night," he lied.

Meg glared at him. Not knowing how innocent he really was anymore, "I never do that." She glared true fire at him, "Look, I've tried to be nice but either tell me the truth or get out."

"You look tired," he scooped her up, though she shrieked in protest. "I'm only going to put you to bed. You look about to fall down. You need sleep," for once she didn't argue she pointed out her room. Let him place her on her amazing queen-sized bed and listened for him to leave.

Meg jumped up when she heard the sound of food cooking. There was a sizzle and the salty sent of bacon. She hurried to make herself presentable. She ran a brush through her waves of hair.

Then she made sure the small swell was covered by her shirt. She stopped when she realized it was Len cooking in her kitchen. "You never left?"

He had the decency to cringe at her tone, "We still need to talk." He should feel guilty all the time she slept he studied her home. It was well built, for a cottage a few hundred years old.

"There is nothing to talk about right now."

"There is plenty.

"Honey, if I were mortal you could woo me to the moon and back. But as it stands the more we talk the more likely more people will know than already do."

He noticed for the first time she had taken time with her looks, "Expecting someone else?"

She shrugged, "Don't get jealous, you have no right. I thought you might be an old friend of mine."

"How old?"

She could only laugh, "Very."

"Demon?"

"Of course."

"Does he know?" Len looked at her thoughtfully, "He doesn't know and would be hurt. The baby isn't his."

"We're not that kind of friends," Meg protested.

This time Len laughed, "Trust a female to think a longtime friend isn't interested in her."

She rolled her eyes, "Only at certain times, as does most of the male population want me. It isn't all that flattering."

"Hope you aren't vegan."

"This is my kitchen and demons eat meat silly."

"Just checking" He served her a steak, some bacon and seasoned potatoes.

She took the seat he offered, "Dinner, then you have to go," Meg demanded.

"Paper and I'll leave you my contact info."

"That isn't a good idea."

"Want to see me tomorrow," He threatened.

"Alright," she relented.

"And don't think of ignoring me. I'll just show up sooner," on that thought she spent the rest of the night with indigestion.

The next day she was surprised by Griff.

"Meglatonlori."

Meg blushed at her full first name, "It's great to see you," she let him in.

Griff didn't have to look at the cottage, he remember helping Meg build it a long time ago, "How is my favorite loner?"

"A-lone."

He hugged her which surprised her. Normally, hugging was reserved for her younger years when she needed a rescue. After time and becoming more self-sufficient she no longer was teased by other demon spawn. She was left alone. Not that she didn't need a rescue now, "You smell different, Megawatt," He pulled away and looked her over.

Her spine stiffened, "I think you are imagining things."

"No pretty," he again searched her for an answer, "You've never come back smelling like this."

"Maybe it is human perfume." Meg shrugged.

Griff kept watch, "You've never came back from breeding season smelling of," He stopped, "You slept with a mortal."

"I have been known to have my fun," Meg reminded, "It is my job." Glad he thought she'd succumbed to a mortal. If he knew it was an angel things might be different. Griff would be proud of her. But then he might want to influence what happened to the life inside her more than he already was thinking. That thought made her turn cold. It seemed the maternal instinct wasn't dead in her after all.

"Who is the lucky bastard," she paled and he said, "sorry." He should have more sensitivity to her feelings, "Do you have details on the lucky guy or guys."

"G," she smiled, "you know me. I don't take men seriously. I just take what I have to survive."

Griff shivered, "You are still a cold one. Even for your kind. Some actually do find love."

She nodded, "It makes my kind a slave."

"A slave?" Griff then remembered, "A slave to have children," she must have flinched because he brightened and dimmed at the same time, "You have a get coming! That is the smell that is different about you." Meg swallowed bile but nodded to affirm his accusation.

Griff patted her hand, "It will get better. Does the poor mortal know? It doesn't matter. If he will not acknowledge the get I would."

Meg jumped in surprise, "You would acknowledge a mortals' get?"

"If the mortal won't."

Meg swallowed at the sacrifice he was willing to make. She knew he cared but not this much, "I do have to give the mortal a chance."

"Does he know the rules?"

"Rules?"

"Rules to dating a demon. I am guessing not. You'll need to tell him of the rule of three. It wouldn't do in your condition for him to call you to him by saying your name thrice. Or calling a higher demon that way either, as his holiness."

Meg turned inward by the thought of the mighty king of the demons, "By all that is unholy, I really didn't think this through."

Griff only gave a belly laugh, "Thinking usually isn't involved in procreation. You of all should know that," He returned to the list, "With you there is also the rule not to outdo your temper. You would flame you and the child to a crisp."

Meg let out a full groan, "This get is going to kill me."

Griff shook his head, knowing she'd died many a times and she came back time and time again. Though unacknowledged, she was of strong demon blood. He sometimes wanted to draw her attention to the clues but he was forbidden. He cursed love and the weakness it made of mortals and demons. He did hope in spite of all that the little spitfire would be rejected by the mortal. Then she would turn to him. He would not mind being called the one to break the unbreakable.

He wondered who the father was but in the city that had grown to be in the millions there is no way of knowing who it was.

Maybe he would have to follow Meg to find out what she fell for. If he was not good enough he would scare the man away. Griff might do so anyway but he would not tell her that. That would be his deepest held secret.

"I'll let you have some time to figure things out for yourself," Griff said, "But if you ever really need me you know how to call me."

Meg nodded, though it wasn't needed. They both knew she knew the ins and outs of being a demon spawn. Though in some ways she felt like an untrained youth. She knew of many places she could go to find the likes such as herself. There were different clubs that were secret demon clubs. But she'd never liked the club scene. She only used it when she had to.

*****

Meg fiddled with her new cell phone options. She'd never really thought to have a phone but things had changed. She needed a phone for her next meeting with Len. She didn't want to face him. The first time had been difficult enough. She really never thought she'd have to meet with a father. She cursed whoever or whatever had set her and Len up. They had to know she would have the power to resist that was why she had been drugged.

Whoever had played the set up knew too much about her. Of course, Len knew too much about her too. That and his threat were what inspired her to get her phone. Meg needed to find out more about what he knew. Though it was the last thing that she really wanted to do was talk to Len.

She wanted the whole situation to disappear. But if her suspicions were true and someone had set her or Len up they would one day feel the demon wrath on them. Sure she would have to have her baby first. Then she would flame on the person that set her up.

Chapter 3

She dialed Len and waited. Before it could go to voice mail he answered. She asked him how he knew her name. He finally admitted that he had a crush on her. Part of her felt settled. Meg wasn't in this alone. He asked how she was doing and she admitted that she was tired and still having morning sickness. Then she asked, "Do you know anyone that would want to set you up?"

"What do you mean?"

"Someone to hurt you. We were locked in that hotel room."

There was a long silence, "No. I can't think of anyone."

Meg rested on her couch. If she were a betting woman, she would say he was lying to her. Why he is lying to her, she could not guess. She almost wished she would have had the courage to face him. But right now, all she could do was phone him.

"Do you want me to come over?" the question vibrated against her ear. She wished she could say yes but she knew Griff was watching her closely as though he doubted, she would do the right thing with regards to the baby. Either that or he was trying to figure out who the father was. That was the last thing she needed, "No. The time isn't right."

Len pouted on his end of the line. Though he was happy she was talking to him. He hadn't thought she would call so soon, "You know, I do know your phone number."

"Yes, I may be an old demon but I do know about technology."

Len laughed, "How old are you?"

"Too old for you," she wished for the old-time phone cord to twist in her fingers. Something for her to do. She was quite too long but Len was lapping up the attention like a puppy, "We do need to meet eventually." Len about fell off his chair. He couldn't believe she would bring it up again, "I need to go to the store today."

"Not going to let your demon friend take care of that. What is his name anyway?"

"It isn't my right to give up the name of another demon. I have to teach you the rules to dating a demon," she mentioned.

"Rules?"

Meg recited what Griff had brought up the other day.

"That is why you don't give out your name," Len realized that was the reason she had wanted to know where he had learned her name. He hadn't realized it was a way to bring her to him. He could understand how the teleportation was not good for the baby, otherwise he would just call her to him.

Instead he would do what she suggested and catch her at the store. She had warned him that some demons frequented it but it was under mortal ownership. So, he, knowing she walked, walked to Jackie and June's. He was surprised when she was wearing sunglasses. Though they were almost falling off her nose. He could only guess it was to help others gage how hot a fire her temper was. Len hoped he never saw the day her temper made her literally go up in flames.

That is when it made the dating a demon more real. Len would not let himself regret getting Meg pregnant. She was in the meat department. He looked in the cart and remarked, "A little heavy handed with the bacon."

"I love bacon." She stated calmly. "Why the meeting?"

"Don't be blunt, it doesn't do well on you." Meg yawned, "I realized that my fridge was empty. Probably because there was a young one at my house." She winked behind her glasses. Len didn't know that he liked her talking about him like that, "Who is your enemy?"

"Enemy?"

"Someone that would be willing to hurt you. I don't know anyone on my side that has anything to gain with me being…."

"From what you lead me to believe any demon would be happy with this situation. So maybe your lovely guardian is the one that did it."

She about said his name, "No my guardian wouldn't do that." Though the seed of doubt was planted. Griff had brought up claiming the child if the father wouldn't step up. If the child turned out to be very special then she'd have to have a different father. A protector would be needed. Meg also recalled how he had smelled the difference in her. Yes, demons had a sensitive sense of smell but could a mere demon smell pregnancy? Now she wished she had someone else to turn to.

Len decided he would have to do some research of his own and find out who her guardian was. Meg might trust him but he would not trust his life or that of his child on a demon he had never known and didn't even know his name. Besides if he was watching over Meg, he should quickly meet up with who would also be watching her.

"What is your name, again?"

Len struggled, for a moment said, "Len." "That isn't your full name."

"Meg, isn't yours either," he argued.

"No but your name isn't as mine." She reminded him, "Now don't think or speak my name again."

"So, my name isn't as important as yours," Len sounded dispirited.

"Pouting doesn't look good on you, Lad." Meg winked at him again.

Len nodded, "So you all call each other different names when need be, M."

"Now you are getting it, Lentil."

"That is disgusting, Megawatt." He didn't withhold his distaste.

Though he did feel free to add items to her cart. "I can't walk all this home."

"Let me help you," he offered.

"It's not that I don't want you to but I don't know what my watcher is doing."

"We are going to meet eventually if things run its course." Len argued.

Meg did a mental calendar of events trying to figure odds that this was the time that G, had different focus. She never knew what happened what he did when he went away. It was probably time that he had to serve for his demon overlord. That was the only thing that was great about be unacknowledged was that she didn't have to slave for an overlord. For all she knew she might have been forced to have a child before now.

That was the problem with having limited contact with other demons was she didn't know what they had to do. Even when she tried socializing with other demons at the club they seemed to close up when they found out she was unacknowledged get. Perhaps it was not only the stigma that kept her solo but also the jealousy of all her freedom.

She sighed, even if it wasn't his time to be away she had little choice but for Len to help her with the groceries, "You win, young one."

Len lost pace with her. He was surprised that she gave in so soon, "This would be easier if you had a car."

"I have plenty of time. I don't need that kind of time machine," Meg answered, "Besides I like the exercise."

Now you have a need for it too, he stopped himself from saying it.

Knowing it wouldn't make her happy. She was more relaxed than he had ever seen her. He wished he could make her feel this free all the time. He wanted to be more to her than just her baby daddy. He was willing to be an outcast in his own world, more than he already was.

Together they walked back to her little cottage. It was hidden from the prying eyes of mortal men. Outside they left it red brick, "How did you luck out and find this lovely place?"

"I was around when it was built."

Len chocked on his on disbelief, "But this place is a few hundred years old."

"I told you, you were but a child." Meg frowned because she hated to know that she had taken advantage of a boy even though in mortal terms he was an adult.

"It doesn't bother me that you are the older woman." He reassured her.

Meg laughed and cried at that, "How you stand by me I don't know." She really didn't. It made no sense. Like her guardian he should have duties to do with being an angel. Though she had to remember his mother had been raped. Even for angels being raped had to be a problem. She would have fallen from grace, "Your father wasn't a demon was he?"

Len was taken aback, "No my father wasn't a born a demon although he may have deserved the title when he raped my mother."

She shook her head something wasn't adding up there was still secrets between them. She should respect his so he would respect hers. For her small panel of friends, she felt as though she was living in a world distorted by lies. What did lies matter to a demon though, she tried to rationalize. Lies were as freely spoken as truth. It wasn't uncommon for demons to live a life of lies.

Len helped her unload her groceries in doing so they did end up touching a time or two. Both could feel the attraction even though the attraction should be gone. Meg couldn't believe there was still a heat between them. "You can't stay."

"I could the damage is already done. It isn't as if---" "Don't even think it or speak it. Anything is possible in this realm."

Len looked as though he could choke, "Anything?"

"Yes, anything." Meg shivered at all the things that could happen just given the thought out loud. Even Len was taken aback. That was something that Meg had not mentioned when there were rules for dating a demon. Of course, she could not remember everything.

"What about the possibility of multiples?'

"One is enough and that is what I have."

Len was glad that she sounded so sure that there was only one baby. That was all he thought they could handle. Multiples would be too much even for an angel and a demon. Especially when she didn't seem to want his help. He didn't understand that she was worried about who had set them up. Len did not really worry, because it was something he had wanted anyway.

Well, if he were honest, he didn't want to get her pregnant so soon.

He wanted to get to know her. Though he knew she was his one and only. That someone tricked them did not bother him. Of course, he could see why Meg was angry. She had been knocked out and drugged. He had only been knocked out.

"Well, it is time for you to go home." Meg responded.

"Since your guardian isn't around shouldn't I watch out for you?"

Meg shrugged, "I can take care of myself. You may have softened me enough to get a phone but don't push your luck."

"You are a tough one, Megawattwatt."

"Very creative but you can't stay."

*****

Griff had been like a child, constantly asking about her and the baby's father. Meg wanted to scream. It wasn't his business. Yet she couldn't throw him out. He might later be needed when she had the baby. Someone wanted this child and wanted it born. The only questions were who and why. There was terrible power to be had of a mixed blood, even when it is mixed with half-breed.

That is probably what kept her silence. It wasn't above her head yet. Hades, there were only three or four that knew she was pregnant. She almost had forgot the unknown person. That was the fourth. She wished she knew the why. Was this something that was even about her? She just didn't know.

"The father wants to meet you too, Griff."

That got the older demon to stiffen, "You told him about me? A mortal doesn't need to know about masculine demons."

"Oh you know you've had a few get in your time. So don't act like you have no relation with mortals."

Griff gave up on the lecture. Meg was one that never did understand the role he played in the demon realm. He hadn't been allowed to teach her and the few demons she used to hang around did not teach her anything. They just belittled her for not knowing her father. It always seemed to come back to her being unacknowledged.

Had she been acknowledged she would be a servant to her father's overlord. Or if he was a high ranking demon she would serve to help him with his needs. Usually that meant having more demon spawn so that he had more lords.

If she only knew how wild she'd grown up. She was anti-purpose but since her father never came forward, she didn't have anyone to answer to. She didn't want to call on Holy Lu because he could order her destroyed. Though she didn't know how she could be destroyed, she'd died different times in different ways and she always came back. She'd been burnt to death and drowned.

"Is that the only way I get to know him, is to meet him with you?"

"The only way you will get to meet him with my blessing."

"Megawatt, you usually don't play games. Is there something I should know?"

Meg just shook her head. She didn't have it in her to say what she had done even though it should be a matter of pride for her. It was probably because Len was not the typical angel half breed. She just didn't want to say it because of prying ears. This was causing her to not really trust. Though she knew she had to trust someone.

Griff just couldn't believe how firm Meg was being. Usually she gave in on everything except of course the one thing now not in her control. The one thing she did not budge on was having a baby. To be honest he was surprised at how well she was taking it. Meg was certainly beyond the acceptance phase. There had to be a reason, which reason he couldn't seem to figure out.

He could not really see the three of them around the table. A table he had helped Meg build. She had liked the original hand carved wood instead of the more modern furniture. He had helped her build everything even the cottage. She had been a young one then. He remembered when she was a child. Griff almost wished she was that girl again.

She certainly kept the cottage up on her own. It was a matter of pride that the city built around the home. It was a hidden little retreat, that people had to know about to find.

"I don't eat with mortals."

Meg felt her eyes turn to flame color but knew that wouldn't threaten Griff. Instead she had to control her temper as he knew, "I have seen you eat with mortals."

"Female mortals."

She rolled her eyes, "Fine don't meet Len."

"Len?" Griff said in disbelief, "That isn't his full name."

Meg nodded, "Like a demon he holds tight to his full name." They did that because if called by the full name they were a slave to the mortal that called them. Whereas if they called by a partial name there was more freedom. Though a demon was still pulled to them.

"I know the father is not a demon." Griff said, "If you were pregnant by a demon the rumor would flood the mills. Instead this is the darkest held secret. What is it you don't want the rest of the world to know?"

She paled, "You've asked about the father?"

"No, Megme, I haven't asked a thing. I just have kept my ear to the ground. Listening for anything even a rumor. No one has said a thing about you."

"By haunted souls, Griff, you about gave me a heart attack." He wondered why she wanted to keep her condition a secret. Something had to be off about the father.

*****

Len listened at a distance. He was right that the demon wanted her. He would have to do his own research on Griff. Demons were usually a prideful on things. The only exception seemed to be Meg. He could understand she was not like any of her kind. Maybe that was why he was so infatuated.

He actually did the unthinkable and followed Griff at a distance. If he were a true angel he knew Griff would smell him out. As it was he would look back puzzled. Griff knew something wasn't right but didn't know he was being followed. He went further into the enchantment that was a demon forest. That at the end had a familiar looking cottage. It was certainly made by the same craftsman as Meg's.

Griff went to the wood block and was chopping wood. His muscles were something to behold. He could certainly crush a man if he wanted to.

As he hacked the wood, he had some creative curses. Ones that Len hadn't heard before. He knew he wouldn't be lucky enough for Griff to be called to his demon master. Len wish he knew the name of his master. That would answer so many questions. But now knowing the way to this forest he would be able to make it back.

Len was on his way back when he decided to call Meg. She told him how she was upset that her guard refused to meet him. He acted surprised because it would not do for him to have her think that he was following her. Actually, he had intended to eat with Meg when he heard the male voice. It did not take much time to figure out who he was.

This time he looked at the house more fully. The furniture was neat but well worn. The cottage was lived in but it was clean. He wanted to investigate her bedroom but knew she wouldn't allow it. That door was sealed shut. But from memory of putting her to bed he remembered it was also tidy. She seemed to notice his direction of his thoughts.

"Tell me about your home," she invited.

"Nothing special just a messy apartment that I rent."

She smiled, "As you get older you find time to clean," she explained about her clean cottage. Knowing at her first years she had found cleaning tedious. It was only when she was older did she find being clean important. That and she about burnt the cottage down, and it was not just her temper that did it.

"You treat me like a child."

"Compared to me you are a child," she said matter-of-factly.

With that he threw his silverware down, "Then you can take care of my mess as you would a child." Having gotten his temper up he stomped out so hard some of the items she had on the walls fell off. Len noticed but he didn't care. He wouldn't go back and help her clean the mess, she was pregnant not helpless and she was trying to hide it.

He walked the miles it was to his apartment. As he said it was messy. There were papers were scattered everywhere. Usually there was one pizza box with an old messy pizza. Len decided he would clean his apartment. He knew it was not for himself but for Meg and the baby. To prove he could be clean instead of being a slovenly mess maker.

Chapter 4

It took a few months for them to get past their fight. Meg had been unwilling to relent and Len was tired of being treated like a child. Even though in some ways he was a child. Meg finally called Len and asked if he wanted to go camping. By now she was six months along.

Len was surprised because she didn't seem the camping type. Until she explained that the camping would be preparation in case they had to be on the run. Since they didn't know the person that set them up they didn't know who was waiting for the baby. They might need to be on the run.

Short notice explained her lack of gear. He wanted to argue but knew she would bring up his age.

She had rented a car to get out of the city so they wouldn't have to walk. But the car would be left at a second rental agency that was in the middle of nowhere. Then they spent the day travelling on foot. Meg pointed out some of the edible foods in the sparse woods. She did it more for his comfort than for her own. He seemed edgy in the unprotected wood.

Of course Len, did not know she had been here before. That Meg had camped here when she and Griff had been fighting. Griff was in a rutting mood and she had not been inclined to help him out. She picked a spot that had a little pond. And unrolled the sleeping bags. They were thin but that was because demons were warm blooded beyond that of humans and angels.

At Len's look of disgust, she mentioned, "You know if you get cold you can cuddle me." Though there were plenty of tall trees to block the wind.

It astonished the angel boy that Meg would invite him to cuddle her. That was the first real closeness they had had since the conception of the baby. They didn't talk much not wanting to anger one another.

Len stayed up until late Meg was already in her sleeping bag. He moved in beside her. She mumbled, "Burnt candy," to acknowledge their combined smell. Then went back to sleep.

He was still disturbed by being out in the open. In the pale moon light he looked at the pond. It was small pool of water that they had stopped by. And wondered if he was dreaming. Because the reflection had Meg with long wings covering the baby and his own smaller wings covering her and the baby. The wings where an indication of their ages. It was on that that he feel asleep.

*****

A white woman held a red baby in her arms while the white crew screamed at her. Her words were drowned out by the yelling of the crew. There were slurs to the woman's character and she only drew her chin up.

"Throw the demon spawn in the water or else we'll throw you both."

Only then did the woman show the weakness of tears, she couldn't let go of her child even if it meant her death. One of the crew plucked the baby from her grasp, "Throw it in the sea or I'll slit its throat."

Then the woman did as told; and threw her baby in the sea. In the sea the baby tried to cry but it couldn't be heard. It was helpless in the long drift to a shore. It could have been days; it could have been months. At the time the baby had no concept of time.

*****

Meg woke and cursed. Not only was she pregnant but the pregnancy was bringing back her memories of her mom. It wasn't what she wanted. She thought she had made her peace with the past but perhaps Meg hadn't. Perhaps there was more she needed to do.

Len woke slowly, "What's the matter?"

"Nothing." Meg lied. And then she felt Len hug her tighter.

As soon as she had calmed down, he admitted, "There is something I need to tell you before anyone else does."

"What is that?"

"You know that my father raped my mother. But what you don't know is that my father was an angel. Obviously ,he decided to fall."

Faster than a viper she turned, "Your father was the angel?!" Len could only nod. "Unmerciful fates! Did you ever think he is the one that could have set you up to fall further from grace?" A shiver ran through her.

A fallen angel was the last thing she had thought of. "Why does it matter?"

"Because your father could use the baby to rise back up. Especially if the child is a mix of all three species."

Len wished he could say that his father would never do such a thing but that would be a lie. His father was capable of anything including using a child to get what he wanted. Of course, he would: he was a fallen angel.

Meg could only shiver and shake. For some odd reason it was easier when she didn't know who the enemy was. Now knowing it was the child's grandfather made her cold. With a demon that is saying something. Usually, a demon felt no chill.

"I know I should have told you sooner. But I was ashamed."

Instead of being angry she could sense his shame and wouldn't let herself be the cause of more shame, "Secrets can be a terrible thing so thank you for telling me."

Len was surprised that she was taking it so calmly. Yet he could feel the chill in her so she wasn't as unfazed as she let him believe.

"Who raised you?"

"His sister. She is the sweetest angel you could ever meet." "Would you trust her with your child?"

"Why should I, there is you?"

"Because if it is part angel, I couldn't claim it." Meg held back her tears, "I'm a soulless demon."

Len said because he believed, "You are far from soulless. You wouldn't care about the baby if you were soulless." Len would defend her to the death if need be she wasn't like any other demon she was special. Meg might be older than the country but she was far from soulless.

"Your mother named you, Fallen, didn't she?" "How did you figure that out?"

"She blamed you for the sins of your father. I can tell by the sympathy you give me." Len was surprised by the lack of judgement in her tone. She was like a different woman. "You don't blame me?"

"No you are still young. Now your father I wouldn't mind hitting him with a ball bat."

Len didn't bring up how she couldn't get a hold of him to do such a blood thirsty thing. Though he could see why Meg would say that. Len had to remember she didn't want to have any children and now she might have one with a bounty on its head. That would be a hell of a change.

"It will be nice if morning sickness ever ends." Meg brought up. "Crackers for the lady then."

She perked up, "You brought some food?"

"I don't go camping unprepared." He opened up his camping bag. He knew her plan had been to walk back to the car rental agency.

It was supposed to be a test night, but he wanted more than one night. It had been nice to have her body in his arms. To feel her soft warm skin. He may have wanted more but he had been content to hold her. Len didn't want to go back to the cold lonely silence between them.

Meg felt happy that he had thought enough to bring something she could hold down. It seemed even though it had been months the symptoms were not getting better. She was one that was sick for longer than average, curse her luck.

Len wanted to ask her to make a deal of no more fighting but that was beyond them. He knew she wasn't ready to not have someone to be angry with. And Len was a prime target. He was the father. He should probably get ready to hear some horrid things about himself when she did give birth.

"It's time to journey back to our homes."

"Does it make sense to keep two separate residences?"

"For now, that is the only thing that makes sense. Otherwise more demons and fallen angels will know about our baby. It would only be more dangerous for the little mite."

"Do you know what it is?"

Meg laughed, "No, but knowing luck it will probably be a boy."

"A boy needs a father."

Meg would not fight the old fight. A daughter needed a father as well. It was only right to know where you come from. Not that life was fair. She was after all the unacknowledged get that she was. It led others to believe he wasn't much of a demon because that is the one thing they flourished in was their get.

"Thinking about your father?"

"What is there to think about? He couldn't be bothered to come forward for me."

"Maybe he couldn't."

"I don't want to talk about someone not worth my time."

Len felt sorry for Meg in that. Yeah, he was ashamed of his father but at least he knew where he came from. Meg didn't know. She sounded like if she found out who he was now she wouldn't be forgiving. Of course, Len didn't know the torment she had live in her first few centuries.

Only now was Meg left alone because she didn't hang out with other demons. Other than Griff. He would only bring up her unacknowledged state when he wanted her to be strong. Or if Griff wanted to see her temper fire out. He did seem to delight in seeing her flamed out.

Meg thought of how hard she had worked to not flame out. It had been ages. All since the baby. There had been a few close calls but it hadn't happened. Praise be to patron saints and silence. Silence had saved her sanity a time or two.

They walked back to the car rental agency they talked of trivia. When they got to the car rental agency Meg let Len drive. He drove her to her cottage. Then he drove the car back to the original agency.

Meanwhile Meg was pacing back and forth like a worrier. She couldn't believe Len had let her stew all these months wondering who set them up. He'd known all along what the possibility was and he was silent. Meg didn't know what she could do next. She would go to Griff but that would involve telling him the mixed origin of her child.

Meg couldn't trust him not to want to use the child as well. It was now a more impossible situation than it was before. Part of Meg wanted to hurt Len. Though she understood his silence. She would have stayed silent as well. Now Meg wondered if she should hunt her enemy or not. She looked down and realized she was too far along to do that. Meg would have to no longer be pregnant to be able to hunt him perfectly.

Meg was surprised how charmed she had been that Len had thought to bring crackers. Although now it was still difficult to eat. Her morning sickness was all day. She just had to guess when it was a good time to eat something. Most of the time she ended up with bad memories and the loathed taste of bile in her throat. She'd drink stronger spirits than just water to kill the bile taste.

She'd tried not eating and that hadn't worked she just threw up stomach acid, which was just as harsh as food, if not harsher. Meg was tired of being tired but she was tired all the time. There was too much time to worry. This baby was taking her to task showing how tough she wasn't.

She took back every curse she'd ever had on parenthood. Except those on her father's head. He deserved those and more. But all others Meg just didn't know. If all pregnancies were this, she didn't see how mortal women survived. Then again in centuries past not very many women did survive.

Elsewhere Len was wondering if he should have told Meg the truth. Now she knew it was his father behind their coming together. He should have known his father would have a negative motive in bringing the two together. Len should have known his father would do him no favors.

The fallen angel was for himself and only for himself.

Would it be another few months before Meg and he spoke again?

Would she now run to Griff? Griff would be a nice strong back and defender. Much more powerful than a chubby angel. The demon was made for fighting.

"Did you speak of me, Fallen?"

Len didn't even show his father the respect of turning around, "Yes I did."

"You didn't tell your breeding demon love did you?"

"Who I speak to about you is my business, Arthenius."

Len felt a cane to the back of his head, "I've told you never to use my full name. If you must use a name call me Art."

Len laughed at his sire, "You having been fallen, are subject to demon law."

"You know nothing of demon law."

"I know of the power of three."

Arthenius laughed, "Playing with demons and that is the best you learned from them?"

"Arthenius, I call to you to leave me."

"How dare you speak to your father like that, Fallen."

"Arthenius, I call to you to leave me," and with a roar Len's father was gone. He knew it wasn't the last he would see of his father but it was enough for now. He didn't want to see him or the demon master he had to have inherited. Since Art wasn't probably free of a master like Meg.

Len knew push presents were new and more for the rich but perhaps for Meg's present he could do something no one else could do. He went to the library of the angels and researched the damned. He wanted to find her father.

There wasn't much of a genealogy, as angels didn't want to account for demon get. Though there were a few fairy tales that were of interest to him. The tales were there to prove that even demons could love that they may have a splintered soul. Something more than Meg gave herself credit for having.

She believed she had no soul and was damned to live forever in the hells on earth.

Len knew right now the tales would only annoy Meg, but perhaps when they were running for real, she would enjoy the tales on the run. Perhaps closer to the end she would find herself in a more romantic mood than she already was. Right now, Meg just didn't seem the type to want to hear of mythical romances even when they involved demons.

She was gritty and a fighter. Because of him and his father she would have to be. One day he would have to thank her for knowing how to get rid of his father without force. All he had to do was command him away three times by his full name.

Len wondered why the same didn't work for him but found he really didn't want to know the technicalities. It would be one step closer to be caught in that trap if he found out. That was something he didn't want to know. That would be his strength, that no one could call him away.

*****

Art soundly cursed his son. His weak, angelic son. He would have to take after his tenderhearted mother and not the father that sired him. No and trust the weak one to go and fall in love with the young demoness. At least she seemed young. Perhaps he was wrong not that it mattered to him in the slightest. Meg was the vessel that would help him climb back up to the towers that he had fallen. The baby would be part angel he would bet his life on it. In fact, he was betting his future on it. If the baby wasn't part angel he would be stuck with the fallen.

Most of them were poor souls that had given up. He would not give up he would claw his way back up even if it took stomping on his grandchild to get there. That is just the kind of fallen he was.

*****

Griff had been trying for months to figure out who the father of the baby was. He found out when the father drives away in the rental car. It took nothing for Griff to go to the rental agency and find that Meg had rented the car but that the father had signed the return receipt. The clerk being a female was happy to show him the paperwork. Sometimes these large cities like New York were just too easy to play people off.

He had a name so he looked it up in the phone book, chancing that he still had an ancient land line. As luck would have it, Len did have a land line that lead to his apartment. Griff stayed away from the man himself not knowing what he was dealing with but the apartment smelled of candy. Unnaturally. That is when Griff cursed. Meg hadn't fallen for a mortal. No, she had to fall for an angel.

This was now a matter of war between heaven and hell. Griff would have to watch her carefully because if he could find out the father was an angel anyone could. He cursed the saints because they were the ones that were supposed to prevent stuff like this.

Trust Megawatt, to be the one to have a first born that was worth a lot to others. Only if the child was demon could he claim it. But he knew, M's luck. She'd have the unicorn child. She wasn't one to make life easy and this baby wasn't going to make the world run any smoother.

Griff wondered if he should make the cottage disappear to force the pair together. But he refused to do that. Not when Griff was still in love with the beautiful Meg. With her inky pool of black hair. Her Native American skin tone since her red skin wasn't as red crayon as most demons.

Griff had other motives for wanting a match with Meg but he couldn't say anything. Especially when she thought of them only as friends. He wanted her more than she would ever know. That her first real conquest was an angel only made her all the sexier. She was dangerous, she always had been.

Chapter 5

Some sense told Meg that Griff knew. Perhaps it was because he had stayed away too long. She knew he watched from a distance. Griff was there if the worst happened but even he had limited powers. Instead of wanting to nest Meg was wanting to run. Fallen had helped calm the urge. But Len wasn't the end all, be all of her life.

Len needed to grow up, which she had to admit he was trying harder than he should for her. It was as though he wanted the one thing they could never have and that was to be a family. They couldn't be much of a family when grandpa was a fallen angel that had arranged the whole affair. Art was the one that had brought Meg and Fallen together for his own selfish purposes. Of course, Meg hadn't softened to her father in law. No, if anything she was counting the days when she would be able to flame him with her temper.

"You shouldn't think such wicked thoughts," Len whispered in her ear.

Meg jumped not only because of the mind reading but just because Len was there. She hadn't heard him come in. He was learning to be sneakier and she didn't know if that was a good thing or not.

"Hurting the grandfather of the child would not be becoming in a new mother."

"Neither is a grandfather using a grandchild to get what he wants. He wants to use the baby to get back up in the graces of the heavens."

Fallen just shook his head, "It won't work. We won't let him hurt our baby. Do you know what it is?"

Meg shook her head, "I can't tell. Sometimes I dream of a girl at times it is a boy."

"Never twins?"

"Hush your mouth. Never that much work praise be."

Len smiled at her demand that he not bring up twins. As though the thought could conjure a mystical twin, "If you like we could move to my apartment."

Meg groaned, "I couldn't live in angel city. Which is the part of the city your apartment resides on." She thought of the sickenly sweet smell and knew she couldn't live in that part of the city. That and Meg would be run out by the full blood angels. They wouldn't be so angelic with a demon in their midst. Not that she could blame them she'd stink of fire and brimstone. It was the way of their kinds.

"At least you know who the problem is."

Meg made a strangled sound, "It was only after you thought it right to tell me."

Len bowed before her, "Forgive me?"

Meg wished it were only that simple yet it wasn't. There was much danger involved with an angel that had chosen to fall. An angel that hungered to get back up into grace. One that wasn't above creating and using a tortured soul to get back up. Its own grandchild no less.

Meg did not respect Len's father, nor did she trust him. From what she had heard was he was out for his own well-being. He certainly had not thought of his son in most of his childhood years.

How else did a part angel fall in love with a demon? A demon that by its very nature used men for her own gain.

Not that that was how Meg liked to think of herself but that is what she was. For once it did not matter whether or not if she were acknowledged.

She still was a sex demon and you just could not turn a sex demon into a housewife. Meg knew that was Len's fantasy to turn her to love him. They could then be a family and love would rule the day.

As with happily ever after, it just was in the fairy tales. There was no way to cure her urge to stray and to use men. Look at Griff, who didn't even have a sexual relationship with her. He still was a slave to help her.

"You muse about your lot in life but what about mine." Len again interrupted her thoughts.

"You are destined to be a protector of this baby. Nothing more nothing less to the demon lore."

"What of the small fact I want to marry you?"

"Why so I can make a mockery of the wedding vows? It is not my place nor my destiny to marry anyone. I am like an alley cat no morals. Just the animalistic feelings."

Len thought for a moment. "You have more moral fortitude than some full-blooded angels I have met."

She sat back in silence, "I feel bad for the quality of life that some of the angels have then."

Len sat in silence because it seemed Meg always had to have the last word or thought on a subject. He could compliment her until he was green, she just didn't know how to take it. For someone with no soul she took control of her environment for her baby. He'd Meg baby proof her cottage. She'd given him things to baby proof his apartment. She knew it was just in case she didn't feel fit to raise the baby.

If the baby turned out more angelic, she planned to give up her rights and let him raise the baby without her. Len felt as though the floor would open up and swallow him whole. He couldn't do this alone. That Len knew for a fact. This is where her barbs about his youth rang true. He was too young to do this alone. Len couldn't protect and raise a child by himself.

Meg of course believed he would go to his aunt for help but she would be hard pressed to help knowing the origin of the mother.

His aunt had been shocked when he had denied himself wings because of the lust he felt for Meg. She would be more than scandalized if she found out he had taken it beyond mere interest. Angels where forgiving but not so very much of their own kind. They tended to hold them to a higher standard of being.

It terrified Len that Meg would even think of letting go of the baby. This he just couldn't do on his own. He would find some way to make her understand he couldn't do this on his own. Meg was not that unfeeling that she would leave her child to suffer.

As he would not let her do it alone where the child a demon. He would live with the stigma. He could deny his birth calling because it really was not meant for him. Perhaps his father really had been meant to be a demon that he now lived as. For Len felt comfortable with the demons more than his own kind.   I   t didn't matter if it was right or not.

"You really shouldn't be staying in my spare room," Meg admonished but could not seem to kick him out. It was nice to have live in company that cooked and cleaned for her. In fact, Len treated her like a princess. That was why she could not kick him out. Len was there when she needed him. He even held Meg's hair when she got sick. It might be maddening when there was no longer a baby to fight over. Then she would either be alone or with her child.

She hadn't thought beyond demon or angel. If it where the special then heaven help her, she would probably need the help of an overlord for protection. That Meg hoped she didn't need. Demon lords were even more fickle than her own type of demon. They were known for their changing minds and high prices for everything. She might have to give her freedom for the safety of the child.

******

Griff went to his overlord. He got so lost in his duties as a servant of his master he almost forgot about Meg's baby. Griff wondered how she had to handle the angel and his attempts to convert her. Griff was sure the angel was trying to save the soul of the soulless. It wasn't until he had a day off that Griff found out Len was the son of a fallen angel. Griff had helped his master with his underlings. It was a job he found joy in.

Then Griff was worried. This news made him even more worried about the whole situation. The baby was the product of two rare hybrids already.

Not many demons were unacknowledged and then there is the son of a fallen angel. He had to get to Meg to make sure she was okay.

He was surprised when he found them in the cottage. "M, you got to take care of you and the little one."

Meg did not yell at him that that was what she was doing. He hadn't been around for so long she had wondered if his master had demanded they cut the strings with their relationship. She was glad she had a demon to turn to.

"You've been tricked he's not just an angel he's—" "The son of a fallen angel. He told me already." "He's still alive. I thought you would kill him."

Meg gave a slight laugh, "I couldn't kill the father of my child. No matter that he did deceive me."

"That is one hell of a deception." Griff couldn't believe how calm she was. She was handling her temper more than he would have expected. Any other time Meg would have been up in flames. Though she had to be calm to not harm the baby, "Do you want me to hurt him?"

"He doesn't need taught a lesson," Len interjected coming into the room, "I've been treating her like royalty since you have been away.

Griff had to admit that Meg looked healthier and happier than he had seen her in a while. It made Griff want to kick himself for disappearing. She was starting to show pretty well. Yet Meg had a genuine smile. Griff could see they had a fragile bond that he had not expected. He thought he could step in and it would be alright. He almost felt sorry for himself but this was not over yet. There was still having and protecting the baby to be done and Griff doubted in Len's power over his own father.

"So how is the little boy doing?"

Before Len could answer he added, "I mean the baby and not his father."

"It's a boy?" Griff nodded to affirm. Meg looked at Len and he looked at her in awe. "You two are making me sick."

"We are just surprised, neither could tell what the baby was," Len explained.

Griff could only shake his head at how hopeless the pair was. They needed more help than they had. He would have to watch the pair because this was something bigger than they are. This is something he might need help with but he couldn't go to anyone with this one. Griff's master would be no help. Griff would have flipped had he known Meg was thinking of maybe going to an overlord to help her. That was the last thing Griff would suggest. The wrong one would use the baby worse than the grandfather was planning to.

"Do you want me to stay?"

"No, I know how to call you if I need you." Meg said with a conviction that amazed Griff. Griff promised himself to watch over her more than he normally would. She needed more watching than she knew.

When he went home, he decided to work on a crib for the baby. He was one that liked to work with his hands when he needs to think. This is what his strong point woodworking. He made sure it was a cherry wood finish.

Griff thought back to when Meg was younger. A young love-to-be picked the wrong time to want to be amorous. She yelled at the young love and then she shot up in flames. Her whole body going up in showers of sparks. That had made the love run away. Griff had patted her down and whispered calming words. It helped her come around

"He picked the wrong time to fool with you M."

"Yes he did now I need to replace my clothes." Laughed Meg.

*****

Little did Griff know that Len was building a rocking chair from a kit. Len needed something to do too that was to help with the baby and build his muscles and strain his brain a little bit. Len thought it would be helpful for Meg to have a beautiful rocking chair. He could see her rocking their son in the chair. It made him follow the directions as easily as he could. Nothing would stop him from gifting it to her.

Meg was also preparing from the birth by keeping active. She knew she needed to be strong of mind and body. Somehow, she knew about the men and their work but she was gracious when presented with the rocking chair and crib. Meg handed out her hugs freely and she could tell that both the men in her life were jealous of one another.

As time got closer Meg knew she could not have the baby alone or with just either of her protectors to catch the baby. She discussed it with Griff and they agreed she needed to be at the hospital. Luckily, he knew a demon doctor in the morgue. Meg hid her apprehension of having her child in the cold, death filled room of the morgue.

It would be a controlled environment that would be safe. At least everyone hoped so. Even Griff had his doubt but he wouldn't tell Meg that would only make her pensiveness worse. And Griff wouldn't do more to make her worse. At this stage worry would only make her go into premature labor and it wouldn't do to have a premature baby. It would be even weaker then and easier for those that want to control it. It just wouldn't do.

It got to the point that Meg lost control of her own house. She had an angel and a demon living with her. One on the couch and one in the baby's room. It was a good thing that Fallen had made the rocking chair it was his bed while his rival slept on the couch.

The men did delight in when she did share the baby kicking. They each of course wanted to feel the power of the little one and

Meg was in no position to deny them. Each time a hand touched her belly the baby kicked as though it was rebelling against being a side show item to be seen. Though the little guy was being felt.

Our tough little guy was all Meg could think. It was almost as though Griff was sharing in this as well, even though he had nothing to do in the creation of the child. Len had finally gotten used to the demon though he didn't like him very much.

At times Meg wondered how they didn't just go out and fight to the death. They certainly both disliked each other enough and they both wanted her. She could almost taste it. It fed her demon hunger for lust. Which was a relief. She didn't want to risk fate and having yet another life in the balance.

*****

It was storming as though the fates knew something was to be mourned. She was in major pain because the baby was coming. She screamed every curse she knew because of the pain yet the baby refused to come. She squirmed on the metal table and could smell the dead. This was not where she wanted the baby to be born but it was safe. Then she saw an angel with a huge knife and he split her open taking the baby.

Meg woke with a scream. The nightmare kept repeating itself. Both men came running to her. She did not want to feel Len's arms around her. Instead she was more welcoming of Griff. "An angel wants to steal my baby and kill me," she cried.

Griff held her, "It was just a dream. You know it won't happen we'll be there for you and the baby."

Meg then turned to Len, "I'm sorry but it was an angel." She shivered in Griff's arms the terror still in her heart and mind.

Len nodded in understanding but it still hurt that she went to Griff. The nightmare was only getting worse. He wanted to comfort Meg but it was impossible with Griff there. And he was always there.

"An angel won't kill you for the baby."

Griff held tighter to Meg, "To kill the baby they might. To an angel the baby is an abomination."

She pulled back and left herself to shiver alone. "That is enough Griff.

You do not need to traumatize the poor boy."

Griff continued, "That is why there are rules for dating a demon but not an angel."

Meg nodded, "We are the more forgiving lot."

Len stood back, "Demons are more forgiving? What are you talking about?"

Griff laughed at his confusion, "Who condones your union? Only the demons. Angels would fall from grace if they saw this mess. Why else have you been reluctant to tell your aunt. Answer, she won't like it. And she certainly would not like the time you have been spending with us demons."

Len wanted to deny it but he could not. Somehow the demons were right. Even though he knew they were the master manipulators of the truth. Rarely did a mortal get a one up on a demon they were the ones that lead to the path of distrust. Len could not say they didn't know what they were talking about because they did know. Len knew there was more they could bring doubt to.

*****

Days were usually better at least Meg did not suffer from nightmares. There were also times that Griff would disappear so that Meg and Len where alone. That was what they needed. At least in Len's opinion. Alone they did things like speak of names for the baby. Now that they knew it was a boy.

That was one thing Len had to be grudgingly thankful for out of Griff.

He had known the sex of the child. Though he was closed mouthed about anything else he may know. It was annoying but that is what they did in secret. Griff knew more and Len could sense it. Though perhaps it was for the best. The more they knew the less they might interact.

Meg got up late as was her habit. She looked at Len with sadness in her eyes, "Sorry about last night."

"Nothing to be sorry about. You were genuinely afraid of angels. I could see where that would lead."

"But you are the father. You haven't wanted to hurt the baby in all this time. Why should I be afraid of you?"

"Demons don't trust angels." Len came closer trying to get a kiss. She slapped him to where his nose bleed, "See you do not trust me."

"Kisses got us into this mess. Trust we don't need a bigger one."
"An innocent kiss. Nothing more, nothing less."

Meg considered it and realized she'd never really had an innocent kiss.

Such a thing was beyond the demon scope. Kisses meant something; they always lead to something more. Looking at Len she knew he wanted to mean an innocent kiss but knew he wanted more. There was always something more added. Where he thought he wanted a simple kiss he wanted more and take more.

"Len you couldn't stop at a simple kiss. So why start something we can't finish."

Len looked disappointed and dispirited, "You don't know where I could stop it and you won't give me a chance. That is what disappoints me is you won't even give me a chance."

Meg felt sad and sorry but she wouldn't give in she couldn't. Not if she wanted to live beyond being an endless mother. To be honest she did want her life back. She wanted to do as she pleased and not worry about anyone else and their feelings. She wanted to look out only for herself and no one else.

Not that that was going to happen. When Meg had the baby if she couldn't keep it she would still worry over the little mite. If she kept the baby her life would never be the same. Then she would have someone that came before her and her needs. That wasn't the life she wanted. That is why Meg had always been so careful.

Of course, she could be a neglectful mother but isn't that what the angels would expect of a demon. That she only thinks of herself. Meg would prove those prudes wrong. Whatever was best for her baby was what she was giving.

"What will you do if the baby is angel?" Meg asked. "We'll raise it same as if it were a demon."

"There is no we in this. I'll be out of the bigger picture. It would be best for baby if I died in childbirth. Later when he is older than yeah, I could meet him but until then there isn't much I could do to be in his life."

"I cannot do this on my own. I won't…"

"You could always take the baby to your aunt."

Len thought of his angel perfect aunt. "I could never trick her into raising a baby born of a demon. She wouldn't hear of it."

"Even if it doesn't have a hint of demon blood in it?"

"You don't believe that will happen any more than I do. We both believe that something is going to happen to where it will have both sides."

Meg had tears in her eyes, "Then you will live up to your name Fallen. You would be forced to live among the demons and live among the lore. Unless the angels are more forgiving than they are made out."

"I could live your life. Or maybe angels are really more forgiving than you think."

"I'm afraid you would be under your father's master. That is the life of the hell-spawn."

Len shook his head, "I don't get it. Why are you so free?"

"I'm unacknowledged get. So, I suffer my shame by myself. With a baby I will probably draw the attention of an overlord willing to take me under his wing. Then I will have responsibilities too."

"Responsibilities?"

"Taking more souls and corrupting them, more than I already do. I will have to have more children so my master has more underlings. Life as I know it is probably over."

"I'm sorry."

"You aren't the one that should be sorry. You were probably drugged like I was. If I hadn't been drugged, I would have been able to control myself around you. Even though to corrupt and angel is a high priority on a demon's list."

"Are there more of us in demon lore?"

"Demon lore is more for the full blooded. I'm sure there is an angel or two that fell for the smooth talk of a demon. They are best at flattery and deception. And in Demon lore the demon always wins. So, it is one-sided at best."

Len took this in. So, demons never wrote down when they lost. That would make demon lore something to avoid when trying to find the truth for Meg. It would be back to the angel files that would have to be his help. Not that he had a way to access demon lore.

Meg had no reason to lie and he had no reason to disbelieve her. She didn't know why he had an interest in demon lore or the history of anything. But if Len were a betting man, he would believe that Griff was the one with the answers. He had always been there for her so it stood to reason that Griff knew more than he let on.

If only he knew the demon's full name to trap him and force him to spill all his knowledge. Instead he could only call the demon to him by deed. All knew demons where liars and tricksters. They did what they had to, to get what they wanted and cared little for anything else.

Len would no more call Griff back to Meg's than he would drink the spiked blood of the demons. Blood itself was a disgusting enough proposition to his angelic constitution but the blood was spiked with other spirits was enough to make Len sick. Angels only imbibed on sacramental wine. That was the only alcoholic spirit that they would admit to taking.

Len knew like demon lore there was some lie to that. Some angels did drink of different types of alcohol. Although there were a few that were alcoholics just on the sacramental wine. So, both histories had holes in it to make the writer the supreme untouchable being they want to present to the rest of the world.

Funny that both sides would indulge in the sin of hubris. That excessive pride that leads to the fall of man. It would probably lead to the fall of demon too. Len knew it was a fault of many an angel. They felt they could do no wrong. They were beyond the free will of humanity.

They were supposed to be dutiful servants of either side that they indulged in. The angels were to promote the good and right. While the demons were supposed to help proliferate the cause of their leaders. Perhaps there was some free will in being an angel or a demon. Though they complained it was only the gift of the mortals.

*****

Len followed Griff to his overlord. What Len learned was Griff was a high demon lord himself. Now why would a high demon lord be interested in the growth and development of a mere unacknowledged get? Len had more questions than he had answers. The overlord was so demonic in looks he hid in a cave and issued orders to Griff. Griff admitted that he was having troubles with his charge, that she was being willful and more than a handful. Griff was careful not to mention that Meg was pregnant. Just that she was being more problems than she usually was. That Griff would have to take time from his other duties to watch over the chit.

He spoke of Meg as though she were a burden to bear. Griff seemed a different demon to his master. Of course, he was more humbled. He spoke with more respect but Griff also spoke lowly of his duty of watching Meg. As though he did not want his master to know his feelings for the girl.

Len wondered at the subterfuge. Why was Griff hiding his feelings for Meg when he left himself plain in the light of reality? Why was Griff acting as though the care of Meg was an unjust burden that he was given? None of it really made sense. He wanted to go to Meg but knew it would only upset her to know he had been sneaking around.

Len was acting more demon than he was angel. Sneaking around like a spy when angels where supposed to be upfront. He would be if that was where the answers where. Perhaps it was time to go to his aunt and deal with her wrath. She was the only one he knew he could trust with the truth.

The angel trooped out of the enchanted forest. He did as Meg did and walked himself back to the angel apartment complex. His aunt owned one of the penthouses. As luck would have it his aunt Ruth was in. He explained the situation to his aunt who didn't pass out as he thought but took the nearest weapon a broom and cracked him in the skull.

"So not only do you have a child coming with a demon you've lived with two of them." Ruth rung her hands, "You'll be taking on their ways and habits the way you are going. You should have come to me sooner. Perhaps we could have convinced the unacknowledged thing to live here."

"Sorry, Aunt Ruth but I tried. Heaven knows I tried. Meg's afraid of many people knowing."

"As well she should. The child could be a key back up to heaven for your father. And you fell quite nicely into his trap." Len would not deny it, "The baby must be protected at all costs. I think that you do not realize what that means." Ruth knew he would do a lot for the child but would he be willing to die for it was another matter altogether. He had his father's self- preservation to deal with.

She kept the other facts he had told her swimming in her mind. There was a legend that it reminded her of…but it just couldn't be. Mortals never ended up getting the better of a demon. And yet if this legend was true, a mortal had won much. Perhaps there was more to legend than a myth that something had happened

She wished she remembered the whole of the legend but it was something that angels and demons both called a tall tell. It was believed to be a lie without a hint of truth. Yet even angels had known to be wrong.

*****

Meg was afraid to be alone but she could do nothing as both men disappeared. She had gotten in the habit of taking a walk with someone with her. She didn't know who to curse for leaving her last. They had promised to watch over her but that wasn't to be.

Not that Len's father would dare to attack her before the baby was born. He would not want to damage the baby.

She thought of calling Griff but didn't want to take him from his over lord. So she did blame Len for leaving. Although she didn't know what angels had to do. Meg just had to put her big girl panties on and be alone. Nothing would go wrong. She was used to being by herself. She was a loner and she needed to go back to that. That is where she belonged. By herself not as a member of a pack.

Chapter 6

Meg wondered how she had ever worried about not having the guys around. Now she had them all around her. Any whimper and they jumped. Of course, she was due any day now. They all wondered when the little boy would be ready to make his appearance. He seemed to know how on edge everyone was for his appearance because he was delaying his entrance into the world.

Not knowing what the child was going to be Meg had not come up with a name for the baby. Perhaps she was just hoping it wouldn't be her place.

That the child would be born only angel and mortal or even demon and mortal. Either would be a blessing both would be a world of trouble for everyone.

She was tiring of the guys nearly getting in a fist fight to aid her first. They rubbed her back.   When she was hungry they would get her something to eat. Not a need went unfulfilled. Most embarrassing of all was when they would help her up to go to the bathroom.

She wished it would end. But as she had little pains she tried to hide it. The men would over react and think it was time. It was not time yet that was for sure. The baby was still up too high. He had not dropped yet.

Meg lay on the couch because the guys simply wouldn't let her do anything. It was annoying to her but she was not raging like she used to be. Only one thing got her rage up when she used to, and that was the danger to her baby. Be it the baby's grandfather or some unknown danger.

"You know the baby may drop if you let me do something."

Griff was the one that said, "The baby knows how long it wants to bake. Why make him come to this world any sooner than he wants?"

"Then you carry him and have him punch and kick your insides." Meg said with an ironic twist because she knew though she may wish it, it could never be.

Len was there offering to rub her belly and perhaps sooth the child within. Meg ungraciously accepted the offer. Knowing the baby would just kick all the harder with someone giving him attention. But she let Len think he was doing well, until the baby hit a bruise with great force and she started to cry.

"He really is ready isn't he, Meg?" Meg nodded with tears in her eyes. "Let us go for a walk."

"Really?" Meg asked.

"Yes, you need some fresh air." Len helped her up and a glowering Griff followed. Len and Meg looked as though they should be a couple. Of course, she was happy on his arm walking. Griff wanted to kick himself for not bringing it up first. It was one of the first times Meg was happy all week.

Especially as Meg led Len to the entrance of his enchanted forest. Griff then suggested they go back. Meg even giggled on the way back. Though by the time they got back to her cottage she was exhausted and fell asleep on her couch.

Len asked, "Are we really going to fight over her until the baby is born?"

"You haven't won yet."

"This isn't about winning or losing it is what is best for Meg and our baby," Len said with authority.

"Do you think you are strong enough for the responsibility?"

"I'll do what I have to do."

"Even your aunt will abandon you." Griff said.

Len ignored the taunt for what it was. He was trying to get Len to give up. Len had come this far he wasn't giving up. Not when it was the girl of his dreams. She shouldn't have that power over him but Meg did.

A week of walks passed before Meg commented that the baby had dropped. He was truly getting ready to be born. Again, she tried to hide the little pain she didn't want to go to the hospital until it was really time. But as time went on the little pains got stronger. "Guys I think it is time."

This time Griff had rented a car. He preferred to be the one to drive.

He could use his charms to allow them to be ignored by the police. He passed several hospitals to get to St. Simon's. Madrid, the demon doctor met them, "Sorry to do this dearie," she had Meg down on a gurney but also had a cover over her as though she were dead. She tossed lab coats to both Griff and Len.

The men hurriedly put them on so they could go down in the bowels of the hospital. Down to the morgue. Madrid added, "It's a good thing that Dr. Johnson the mortician is out sick tonight."

Once in the morgue they let Meg be uncovered. She was feeling she had been here before. It was difficult not to let the feelings of the dream come in. Instead of cursing she screamed letters to every alphabet she knew. By the end of that tirade her water had broken and the baby's head was crowning.

Madrid also didn't like the smells of death in the morgue but it was the only safe place for the baby to be born. She didn't like how long it was taking. She didn't like that they could not have a baby monitor but this birth certainly couldn't be on the books.

Meg lost consciousness, she felt as though she were in a dream. A voice said, "All you ever wanted was a soul. You could have one now."

"But the baby-"

"Are you willing to die for him?"

Meg knew what had to be done, "I would die for him."

Meanwhile as she committed to dying Len was holding her hand and felt it go slack. Griff and Madrid both cursed as they went to attend to the baby. Madrid pulled the baby out and he gave a lusty cry.

Len couldn't feel joy not when Meg was dead. He felt empty and alone. He couldn't do this alone. He didn't want to do this alone.

Griff and Madrid both cleaned the boy and agreed that yes it was going to be a lot of trouble. He was one quarter angel, one quarter demon and half human.

"How can you go on as though nothing has happened? Meg is dead."

Madrid patted his hand, "You don't know much about demons do you lad? Give her a little time she'll revive."

Len looked at Madrid as though she were crazy. Dead was dead wasn't it? There was no revive in it for Meg. That is when Art tried to sneak in and grab the baby. That is when Griff jerked him away from the baby. "Fallen send your father way."

Len was speechless with Griff. He could not seem to say anything in his grief. Griff let out a vile curse then proceeded to beat Art to a bloody pulp.

It was to the scent of death and blood that Meg came out of it. She did not scream when she noticed that Griff had beat the fallen angel to where he could not stand on his own two feet. Meg further assessed that Madrid had the baby and that Len was stupefied. Meg got up and she got her own personal punch into the mix.

Len fell back when he saw Meg get up, "What part of soulless demon did you not understand?" Griff verbalized to Len.

Art finding an opening crawled out alone. He knew to get out before the only one to bind him away got his wits about him.

Meg got her baby from Madrid, "Your short name will be Storm." "Don't I get a say?" asked Len.

"Not when you couldn't speak when you were needed most." "I thought you were dead-"

"And your father would have taken the baby if it wasn't for Maddy and G."

"I didn't die for our son just for your father to take it and use it to scale up to heaven," Meg yelled.

To that Len didn't know what to say. He had been so filled with loss he hadn't cared about anything or anyone else. Even his own son.

Meg's eyes were molten but she didn't flame out, "I guess I cannot flame out anymore."

Griff was stunned, "I've never heard of that before." He looked at her, "Is it possible that you now have a soul."

"I'm not gonna kill myself to find out that is for sure. All the more reason I need to have someone to protect me." She shivered, 'No offense to your friend but I would really like to leave the morgue."

Madrid smiled, "No offense taken. You have a beautiful and special son."

Griff grunted and hugged Madrid, "Thanks for your help."

Griff drove the brooding couple to the cottage. He knew he could stir the pot but didn't. Not when Griff was sure he could do a better job than the young Len. He still had his duties to his over lord. Whereas Len was free.

He was scared that Meg was now presenting mortal traits. It could be a detriment to her and little Storm.

An exhausted Meg gave the baby to Griff to watch over him. He knew he should be honored but he didn't know if he should be. Perhaps he was scared of the angel in the baby. Angels always tried to convert the unconverted.

Len meanwhile sulked in the living room. He had been denied access to his son since he had almost let his father take the baby. He felt shame a mile wide. It was more than he could help to take in. He thought about leaving but only stayed because Griff might disappear.

*****

51

Griff placed Storm in the crib he had made. He made himself sit in the rocking chair Len had made. It was a point of being that he liked to use handmade furniture. This out of the box stuff was beneath him. He'd have to make one from scratch later. Griff didn't feel bad that Len was in the negative light he was in. He had earnt it. If not for Griff and Madrid, Storm would be lost.

Griff looked at the little mite. He was still angry red infants usually are after birth. He counted the fingers and toes, though he knew Meg had already done it. The only thing Griff could find fault in was that the child was a quarter angel.

There were no marks that the child was demon but Griff could smell it, it was a burnt candy smell. Not a strong one since he was after all half mortal. It would be interesting to see how the non-mortal sides of his DNA would affect growth and development. Griff drifted off wondering if he would be taking on the father role or not.

Meg awoke a little refreshed. Death took a toll on a demon; it would seem more so on one that had given birth. She went to Storm's room and smiled at Griff who was at first asleep and then alert at the intrusion.

"Saints never said this would be easy."

Meg nodded, as she realized nothing was ever going to be the same again. She was now in love with the target of the underworld. He was an untapped source of power. Meg could not let anyone get Storm, "I was hoping."

"What about Fallen?"

"I just do not know anymore."

"He was supposed to stop his father. Instead he stood there." "I know, Griff, it was a rookie mistake."

"But remember he is a rookie."

Griff growled, "I think you care about the irritating angel spawn." "And if I do? I mean he is Storm's father." Meg growled back. "Forget about the angel and join with me."

"As what, the wife of an under lord? That isn't a very glamourous life."

Griff ached to tell her more but he was bound by demon law. If she only knew, she might make a different choice. But he was bound as she was to being unacknowledged.

"Dare I ask what you fed my child while I was dead to the world?" "Human formula. I did not need him getting sick on me because he cannot handle demon wine."

"At least you did one thing right." She teased him. "I can do more than one thing right." Griff assured.

"Oh stop it. Go sleep in my bed and get some real sleep."

"You won't need me?"

"I think we got it, G. If not, I know how to wake you."

"Thanks, I think, M."

Meg changed her son and took him to see his father. She was still cross with Fallen and he knew it.

"Do I get a second chance?"

Meg looked Fallen full on, "Yes there is a second chance. But next time you better not freeze up."

"I won't Meg, I promise." "Don't," she cautioned.

"You aren't pregnant anymore."

"Doesn't mean I want to be bound to do your bidding."

Len shrugged, "What demon wants bound? I can't think of one."

Meg nodded her assent. There was no need to verbalize more on that account.

*****

Griff nodded at Meg and dismissed Fallen. They had lived together for a while now. The addition of Storm was just another mouth to feed. He was also the reason they were together. Griff swore being around an angel was making him soft. Meg just rolled her eyes.

"I don't think father will attack here."

"Not from a lack of wanting to," Griff stated plainly, "I've made some fortifications."

Meg nodded, "At least there will be one place safe for everyone." "Safe for only little S."

"That is who matters most," said Fallen for Meg. Meg was silent, "Someone is calling me."

Griff knew, "Fallen's father no doubt. Be strong Meg."

*****

"I call to you, Meg." Art said with emphasis. "You summoned me." Meg said with venom. "I did, you have to do my bidding."

Meg kept from rolling her eyes, "As you bid." Art laughed, "I want you bring your son."

Meg arched her brows, "You want me to bring my son."

"Yes, you stupid demon slut."

She said, "So shall it be." She left him on foot. She did not figure he would follow her. He was sure in his ability to have her at his command. It took a few hours but she got home. Fallen opened the door.

"He commanded me to bring my son. He did not say where, he did not say when." She said robotically to Griff.

"Let's take the little mite to see his grandfather then." Griff found an unlocked car and found the keys. Stealing was more the demon way after all. He had Meg sit in front with him in case she got called away again.   He let Len sit with Storm. They didn't speed they took the trip gently. Meg giving directions.

When they got there, they honked. Art came out cursing, "You were supposed to bring my grandson, you arrogant slut.

Meg rolled down her window with her eyes a burning red, "I did bring him." Instead of her going up in flames, flames shot out of her eyes. Art howled in rage as he burned.

Art rolled in the ground to extinguish the flames howling like a tortured spirit. He sputtered as he came back up, "You are supposed to work for me."

"Silly fallen angel," Griff laughed, "A demon always does what is best for them. We brought your grandson so I think you should release, M."

"I release you Meg, but don't think I will stop."

Len got out of the car. "I bind you Arthernius, I bind you Arthenius. I bind you Arthenius from hurting your grandson."

"Fool. I will find a way to get what I want and that child is mine. Mine by blood, mine by right. If I can't get him there will be others. You think I am the worst enemy you have you'll have to run."

Griff got out of the car and beat Art to a pulp. "See who your grandson has in his quarter."

Griff drove them back home. Each had their own set of worries. It was easier to have the enemy you know then the enemy you don't know. But they would weather through the hardships. They were all enamored with little Storm.

Griff stopped asking Meg to marry him because he knew it was no use.

She refused because she was partly enamored with Len. Surprisingly he hadn't offered to marry her. Perhaps he feared her refusal. No one knew but Len.

Len was keeping close to the vest. He wanted to marry Meg but he was afraid she would outright refuse him. It was bad enough that the union wouldn't have his aunt Ruth's blessing. But to hear the potential bride say no was more than he could bear.

Meg wondered why Len had lost interest in her. Soon it would be time to go away again. She would have to trust Len and Griff to take proper care of Storm. Never in her imaginings did she ever expect a demon and an angel to get along well enough to take care of her son. Of course, in her imaginings she had always been childless. It was strange how the world worked.

Now that she was a mother; she couldn't imagine life without her Storm. But she certainly didn't want anymore. One child was more than enough. Especially when they had to be on the lookout for those that would use Storm for their own purposes.

Griff knew when she was leaving, though poor young Len just didn't understand. Griff had to explain rutting season among demons. That was when Len offered to go with Meg. Meg didn't like his smug attitude or his belief that he could impregnate her again and there would be no consequences.

Meg made sure he knew in uncertain terms she was not to be followed. That as usual she would take care of herself as she saw fit. She hated leaving her baby but knew it was for the best. He did not need a sister or a brother.

One was more than enough to worry over.

The men did the best they could being alone. They had formula but of course Storm wanted only his mother. He would not accept anything else and so went to sleep fitfully.

Griff said what he thought, "You know she might have stayed if you would marry her. Then she would have a commitment of a life partner." "If you believe that why don't you marry her?" Len pried.

"I would but she won't do it not when the child and responsibility is not mine."

"You have asked her and she has said no?" Griff only nodded in the affirmative, "Yet you think she would say yes to me? Are you crazy? I have less to offer her than you do."

"Trust me she wants you."

"Wanting isn't enough. What of love?"

"I'd say she loves you more than words can express. Would you trust me? I've known her longer than you have and she wants to marry you,"

"Wouldn't she have stayed if it was true?"

Griff laughed, "Don't you know her she wants her privacy and she wants as few children as possible."

"Demons have breeding seasons?"

"As do all animals. She just chooses to go above that calling."

Len thought of that and realized what a prize he was wasting. He'd wanted Meg since he could remember and all he had to do was ask for her to marry him. Perhaps it was pathetic that he didn't want more but he didn't.

All he wanted was in reach. Well, maybe, he wanted a few more kids but he was sure once married that could be negotiated.

Only he had the long wait before he asked her. She was gone so long that Griff had had to report to his warlord. Thank the saints Meg wasn't so condemned. Perhaps it was wrong of him but he could only see the good in her situation of being unacknowledged get. She had no master only herself to answer to.

Even Griff had stopped acting like the overbearing father that would not let his daughter marry such an inferior being. Indeed because of Len's youth they thought of him as less than they. Not something Len liked to look at but it was the truth.

Chapter 7

Meg had learnt a lot about herself since she left the guys. She no longer wanted to be the independent one that she used to be. She loved her little family but knew that Griff and Len couldn't be expected to coexist forever. They were meant to be enemies. Meg had to figure out how to let one of the men go.

If Len didn't want to be a family then she would turn to Griff. It was only right that the father of her child get first rights. If Len no longer wanted to have the corruption of tainted blood then she would ask Griff to be her partner and all it entailed. Meg didn't doubt that Griff would say yes to her. Not when he had always been there for her. This was something different.

But having learned what she had in the past year; she knew Griff would take her whichever way he could get her.

It made her tingle to know there was someone there for her no matter what. Somehow it made Meg feel free. If not for Storm she would really feel trapped but he was her little miracle. Even with his dangerous quarter angel blood he was her marvel.

Meg wished she could always feel this good and this in love. Storm's unconditional love was more than her little heart could bear. Being part- immortal, it might be longer before he was causing her trouble and declaring that he hated her. That would be later for now Storm was just her baby boy.

It was true what they said children were the center of your world. It was a love she didn't expect and at one time didn't want. Now she couldn't imagine life without her little Storm. It tore her to be apart from him. But Meg didn't want another baby so this was the way it has to be. Though there were times she hungered just for a hug. At this time that was one of the more dangerous cravings. At least as soon as this season was over, she could see her little boy,

No one probably wanted her home more. Storm certainly wouldn't understand why she was gone so long. The one that truly understood her and her eccentricities would be Griff. He'd dealt with her for centuries. It just mystified her that she hadn't realized Griff had been truly interested in her.

She had always thought he was joking when he brought up any relation between them. It just seemed so silly.

Now it hurt that she was hurting him but she would be true to her feelings. She would see if Len really wanted to fall from grace and take her as his wife. Somehow Meg just could not see him saying no to her. He had been in love with her from the word go and she just didn't see how that would change. It couldn't change.

She returned to her home to find only Len. He was asleep in the rocking chair he had made and little Storm looked at her with devilment in his eyes. Before she could stop her son, he let out a large scream that awakened Len, "Meg, you are back."

"Yeah, I know nature can be a long undertaking. Did G get called away?" Meg asked wondering why she didn't see her old friend.

Len was disappointed that her first question was after Griff, "Yeah he got called away." His face even showed it.

"I should have thought as much. You kept Storm in while Griff was away?" She asked with all concern for her son.

"Of course, since I don't know the nature of the enchantment of the house." Len answered in annoyance.

Meg took in the information and nodded, "You did very well." "Did I?"

"I would say so Storm is safe and happy. That is what matters the most in this situation." She affirmed.

Len was quite for too long. "There is a situation that I want to bring up."

"What would that be?" Meg asked.

"I would like to know if you will marry me."

Meg paled in first blush of shock, "Are you sure you want to marry me? This would complete your fall from grace?"

"I love both you and Storm. I want to be the one you turn to for protection." Len said in spite of potential protests.

Meg did bring up her solitary concern, "You won't have me kick G to the curb."

"Hades no, our son needs a demon uncle to take care of him." Meg purred, "Did I ever tell you that I love you?"

"No ma'am."

"Well, then let us start with now, I love you."

Len was to the moon and back he couldn't believe the woman he loved, loved him back. Especially when he was a flabby little angel spawn and she could have a god like demon.

That had to be true love. He couldn't ask for more, "I'll have to tell my Aunt Ruth."

"Don't expect my warm welcome into the family," Meg warned. "Ruth isn't like that."

"Ruth is an angel. She may have a fallen brother but she is true angel."

"She might surprise you."

"The only angel that has surprised me is you," Meg declared honestly.

It annoyed Len how narrow minded Meg could be. He could see it of a regular demon but she had had a liberal upbringing. It showed in how she could control herself. She acted as though she had a soul she wanted to protect.

Len called his aunt to tell him they needed to talk she agreed.

Thinking it was a grand idea. He told her he would meet her in a few hours because he wasn't at his apartment. She hummed that she knew this and had wanted to speak with him for a while. Though she was an angel she had a reporter streak in her. She seemed to know everything.

Ruth was a graceful beautiful angel. With dark hair and pale green eyes. She was everything her brother was not. She was reserved and not a hint of danger seemed around her.

"What is it you wished to speak about?'

"Aunt Ruth, I am in love."

"I can only wish it was with a nice girl. Not the half demon that you have been in lust after."

Len felt slapped, "You don't approve of her. Then you will not approve of the rest. We have a son. Who is one quarter angel and one quarter demon?"

"Now I remember," Ruth intoned, "Yes you went to live with the demons. Have you come back to spew their ways at me?"

"Actually, I came because I asked Meg to marry me."

"You've done things a little backwards don't you think?" Aunt Ruth reprimanded.

Len blushed at his aunt, "It wasn't an accident, your brother was the one that got us together and if Meg hadn't been drugged it wouldn't have happened."

"You are telling me the girl has the self-control to bypass her demon urges." Aunt Ruth said with more than a little disbelief.

"Yes, Aunt, I am because she just got home from being away during one of her seasons. She wants only one child."

"And her overlord will allow this?"

"She has no overlord. She is unacknowledged get."

"Sounds as though she is a rose among the thorns. I shall have to meet her before you marry."

"So, I have your blessing, Aunt Ruth?"

"Only if you don't marry as Demons do, they have loose relationships." Ruth replied in all honesty.

Len looked almost fallen, "I want a true marriage."

"It will be a difficult road for you. You are so young. It isn't what I wished for you."

"I know Aunt Ruth, but all will be well." "And I'll want to see my great-nephew."

Len said, "Then come with me. So, he will be protected by magic from those that father would run his mouth to. Since I did bind him from using my son."

Ruth bit her lip, "Binding is a demon trait. I think I will go to see they aren't teaching you all manner of sin to get used to."

*****

Meg mumbled a curse as she smelled the candy of a full-blooded angel. Until she saw Len with who must be his Aunt Ruth. Then she opened the door with a surprised expression.

"Forgive me for not giving notice but my nephew was adamant." Meg laughed, "Fallen wants what he wants."

"What he wants my dear is you. By looking at you I can see the attraction."

"Thank you, I think. Do by means sit at the kitchen table."

Ruth carefully took her seat and said, "Thank you, my dear. I notice that you don't have a lot of the modern distractions that rule the day."

Meg was impressed, "Yes I only have a phone because of Len. I like the quite life. Or at least I did," she chuckled as Storm started crying, "Let me bring you, your great-nephew." She went to the bedroom and brought her freshly cleaned son down.

Ruth looked at how she shown with love for her child, "This changed everything didn't it?"

Meg nodded then added, "I never wanted children but now I would die for him again and again."

They explained about how she had died when he was born and how Art had almost gotten his hands on the baby. How if it wasn't for the demon help the child would have been used for Art to storm the gates back into heaven.

Ruth cringed to hear so heartily negative of her brother. She had always secretly hoped he would redeem himself instead of becoming more like the fallen angel he was. She hardened her heart and had to learn what a drain the man was, "Fallen is like the son I never had. Now it looks as though I will have a daughter too."

Meg nearly dropped her hold on her son, "You cannot mean that." "Of course, I do. You have a hold on poor Len's heart."

When Ruth offered to hold Storm, Meg carefully handed the baby to Ruth. Storm being the naughty little boy he was he pulled on Ruth's ear lobe. Instead of crying out she laughed at the child being so rambunctious. "You two are going to have your hands full."

Len was the one that took Storm from Ruth, "I'd almost want another one but I already know what mama has to say."

Meg's eyes looked about to shoot fire, "I think one and done is more than enough."

"See what I mean?"

Ruth could only laugh, "You two will have a lot to work on if you truly are going to get married."

"The vows will have to be more than death do us part. Death is easy for me. I just come back awhile later." Meg mentioned.

"We'll discuss that later, "Len found himself putting it off for his own reasons.

Ruth nodded, "I think you two might have a shot after all. Remember to invite me to the wedding." She made her goodbyes and it helped them all.

The trio sleep well into the night.

⚜⚜⚜⚜⚜

Griff was surprised when he heard the pair where marrying with the blessing of Len's aunt. He'd hoped for some tension. As it was, Griff was feeling as though he was being replaced. Meg would no longer need him. She would have Len there for her. A boy when she should want a man.

Instead she enfolded Griff in a brief hug and said, "What would I do without you?"

"Live happily ever after?"

Meg laughed, "That is for fools. We know you'll still be needed around. You are much better at fixing the house than Len will ever be. You are after all the one who built it."

"You built it too."

"Don't tell me that my marrying, I have to give my G up. I really couldn't stand to hear that."

"Well, I don't think your husband will like it."

"If I can't have my uncle Griff then I don't want to get married."

Griff chucked at Meg's adorable pout. She certainly knew how to get her way, "Who could say no to that face?"

Meg smiled and the world was back to the way it should be. Though Griff did exit the house to leave the pair to learn to live together. Which was more of a trial to Len than he thought it would be. Of course, he expected to room with Meg. She, of course, refused pointing out they already had one child. They didn't need a second. And they didn't need to live in sin as his aunt would say.

It was the last part that got to him. He didn't want to offend his aunt. But he was still a man and had his urges. He didn't understand that Meg fed on his feelings of want. That is what got her through without any physical contact. That was something she had developed over the years.

The couch was getting uncomfortable. Oh, how he wanted to share the soft bed she had. To languish in the feel of flesh being warm next to flesh. He stopped himself. His thoughts were getting him into trouble. He didn't know that Meg already knew and was delighting in them in secret.

Perhaps planning the wedding would be more of assistance to him. They could not have a church wedding because his bride was demon. But they could have it outside in a beautiful area. She wanted it out in the open field. Which there was no such thing in the big city. Unless she meant the path to Griff's. He did not want his marriage to begin on demon ground.

Though demon ground would be cheaper than renting a space. The idea was beginning to grow on him though he would never admit it to Meg. Then the mixed wedding would become more of a demon wedding.

Which sounded like a contradiction of terms but Griff did affirm to him that demons did bond. They may not stay faithful but they did marry. That was one thing Len was firm on that Meg would only turn to him or there would be no marriage. He would not entertain her plying her nature with any other male or baring a stranger's children. No if she married him Meg would bare only Len's children.

Meg had returned that there would be no other children if she could help it. Which Len had just laughed. If she though once they were married that they would not be fruitful and multiply she had another think coming. In his mind Storm would not be an only child. He intended on at least one more. Just not in the near future.

He would have to woo Meg from her current mind set. Surely, she would see the sense of having more than one child. Otherwise they would end up with a spoiled brat. Of that Len was pretty certain. Storm was already showing some tendencies of being spoiled. Especially when his mom was around.

Not that Meg could see it, she was too busy being the nurturing mom to notice how bratty he was becoming. Storm was coming to run to Meg or Griff because both were really too indulgent. Len did not know that was the nature of demons to be indulgent to the youth because after youth there were responsibilities that demons usually could not get out of. Barely out of childhood they would have to take seriously the responsibilities of their over lord.

Meg was just trying to let her son have a fun babyhood and childhood. She did not want to be one of those parents that crushed the spirit of her child at the first. And Storm was just the normal dirt playing little boy. That yes did not want to wash before dinner. That drove Len to nearly drink. While Meg would just accommodate by just washing him with a cloth. He was still young after all. He was not even one yet.

Len still felt Storm need more respect for his rules. He followed the indulgent demons to the letter and yet the little boy would disrespect his father. It was a bone of contention for Len.

"You are too harsh with him. He is just a baby." Meg would say to remind Len to soften up.

"You are too indulgent with him. He will grow up to be a pig."

Meg just shook her head and went about parenting as she did. She did not show an interest in Len's way. He was too harsh for a toddler. You would have thought he was raising a small angel. Len was forgetting the child was more mortal than anything else. He was almost a tyrant when it came to his son.

Meg had come to focus on that instead of the wedding because she had no idea who could give her away. Griff was her first thought but he would rather keep her than give her away. She could see him trying to run away with her. That wouldn't make for a good wedding.

She thought of asking for Ruth's number and running the idea past her. Perhaps his aunt would be willing to take up the role or know someone that would be good to give her away since she had never known her father. The unacknowledged get thing was rearing its ugly head up once again.

Meg cursed circumstance soundly. How could she live the life she wanted when she was on her own in so many ways? She had no family, which is why she was so free with Storm. She didn't want to push him away even though he was so small. He was the only true family she had.

Len could not and would never understand that. That is why he was pushing for a perfect child. That was something that did not exist anyway. He needed to understand that the child would be a child and would test limits and boundaries. Though there needed to be limits and boundaries they didn't need to be so tight as to choke the child off.

Len asked time and again for a wedding date but the longer they waited the longer Meg seemed to want to wait. She'd lived many a lifetime but he had not. Compared to her, he had barely lived at all. He was asking a big commitment of himself and of her.

Meg was wondering if he would have second thoughts later on. He might wish he had had more of a childhood himself.

She would have to get all her gratification out of him or from the lust of others. But no direct contact with another male, at least in the sexual realm. That was asking a lot of her. She was used to being fancy free and answering to no one. He didn't seem to understand the transition was taking time for her.

Meg was feeling out what it would be like to see if marriage was the right avenue for them. She had said yes, but that seemed a lifetime ago.

Things were different some of the new had rubbed off. Making the commitment not seem as fine an idea as it was before.

Meg knew her one child limit would go out the window with a husband. He wouldn't allow her to spend every rutting season away. There was no way to prevent at least one more child. But she would refuse to be one of those forever pregnant waifs. No, she would have a mind and she would have some control of her body. That was only right.

"Are we ever going to set a date?" "There are things that are still unsettled." "Such as?"

"Who will give me away?"

"At the rate we are going Storm can."

Although the sarcasm burned, Meg liked the idea but knew that Len would never wait that long. "Any other ideas?"

"No, I honestly know Griff would take you away and never give you away."

"That is what I was thinking."

"Do you really need someone to give you away? I mean you have stood on your own, you don't need someone to give you away." "Doesn't mean I don't want to be given away."

"Any old lover?"

Meg hit him in the back of the head, "That is disgusting."

"I was grasping at straws like you are. I just want the wedding over with. So, I can sleep with you again."

"It was nice until you added the last part." "I'm a man not a mouse." Len said.

Meg just rolled her eyes.

Chapter 8

"Ruth, we are at our wits end." Len said with no exaggeration at his aunt's apartment in the city. "To call me in you must be."

"Meg wants given away but there is no one." "What of her demon under lord friend?"

"Friend yes. But he seems more of an overlord. And a powerful one
at that."

"You have a problem with that, Len?" Ruth asked.

"Why does such a powerful over lord care a wit about a stray demon?"

"Normally, demons do not bother unless it is their own." Ruth observed in musing.

"Are you saying she is related to-"

"One that may not wish to be named. There is a legend. But you didn't bring Meg so I don't feel comfortable speaking of it now."

"Meg still has problems with angel apartments." Len argued. "Something she will have to get used to married to an angel." "She likes the privacy of the cottage."

"Of course, she does. But once married you'll have more protection at your apartment."

"I don't think Meg sees angels as fighters."

"A demon wouldn't." Her lip turned down, "If what I think is true the cottage may be stronger protection though I hate to admit it. I just hate my great-nephew growing among the demons."

"I worry about that too, Aunt Ruth. Ruth why don't you come visit. I think Griff is away." Len knew that Ruth wouldn't be comfortable around Griff.

"I'll drive since I own a car." Ruth nodded. Referencing how demons didn't normally own things like cars. More often than not they stole them. Len watched as the distance was gobbled up. It was so much less trouble than walking.

At the sound of a car Meg opened the curtain. She breathed a sigh of relief when it was Ruth and Len. Meg fussed with the house and said she wished she would have gotten a call before they arrived so she could tidy up the house.

Ruth just laughed, "A happy house with a child is always messy."

Meg agreed to that whole heartedly, "What brings you to my cottage?"

"Len and I were talking about the wedding." Aunt Ruth said. "What were you talking about, should I be afraid to ask?" "Your biggest wedding problem."

"Oh, who to give me away." Meg said in dead tone. "To which I brought up your demon friend." Ruth said. "A demon under lord?"

"More like overlord," Len answered. Meg looked at Len as though he was growing another head, "I followed him."

Before Meg could say anything, Ruth added, "There is a myth my dear."

"A myth?" Meg asked.

"A myth that one time a human did get over on a demon. Not any type of demon either but a demon lord. They were lovers hundreds of years ago. She became pregnant and asked for one thing of him. Thinking it would be a silly boon he agreed. She asked that he never acknowledge the child. So that she may have the life she choose. Instead of suffering in servitude."

"I've never heard of that one."

"One where the demon loses, I would think not." Ruth said in all honesty.

Meg's head was spinning, "You are telling me my father is a high demon lord?"

Ruth nodded.

"And G, the man I have trusted all my life is really is overlord? Do you realize how outrageous you sound?"

"How else could your father protect you he couldn't give you a name so he sent one of his best men." Ruth explained.

"That's why Griff would never tell me much about his master," Meg mused. The more she thought about it the more that it really did make sense.

"He would have to trust him the most, he who would not be named." Aunt Ruth continued on.

"No wonder, he never made a move on me. I always wondered why.

When it was so obvious that he wanted me. Things are making sense." "But knowing the truth do you still want to marry me?" Len asked.

"I do. Now I feel safe knowing the power that is in protecting me and my family." Meg said with confidence.

Griff came in, "I thought I smelled angel."

"Don't be crude Griff." Meg said trying to reprimand him. "We were telling her who her father was," Len bragged.

"Oh really?" Griff said with a laugh, "Two angels figure out what all of demon lore couldn't."

"It involves a mortal pulling one over on a demon. So, of course, it wouldn't be in demon lore." Ruth said proudly.

Griff paled, "You believe this nonsense Megawatt?"

"It would explain why you never hit on me hard. Why you waited for me to come to you, which never happened," Meg said reluctantly.

"I wanted to give you free will."

"You didn't want to offend my father." Meg snapped back.

"Rape is not something that is frowned on in the demon world. You are thinking like a mortal." Griff said reminding her of her kind. It really wasn't uncommon for rape. Griff had certainly had the opportunity. He had never taken advantage of his role in Meg's life. For that she could be forever grateful.

"I am half mortal." Meg said with a passion. She wanted to remind him.

"To that there is no doubt." Griff said.

"Don't you want to apologize for lying to me?"

"I had to lie to you." Griff said.

Ruth said, "He had to obey his master. He still does."

"My master isn't going to be happy you figured out about him." Griff reminded.

"Griff, as long as I have been alive, you don't think there is an expiration date on a promise?"

"It wasn't me and it wasn't my promise." Griff reasoned, "Who am I to judge? I am humbly the servant not the master."

"My mother has been gone a long time. Almost all the mortals call my life. She threw me overboard for the love of—"she fumbled for something to say in mixed company.

"Your mother threw you overboard?" Len said in disbelief.

"It was throw me overboard or the ships' crew would have threw us both overboard. So, I understand. Throwing me over didn't hurt me but she would have died."

"Still, it is your mother." Len protested.

"I told you, you wouldn't understand my truth."

Ruth nodded in sympathy, though to an angel she didn't understand it either.

"Unfortunately, it is a true romance between the two," Griff said dead pan, "He still loves her."

"That is sick." Len said.

"He loves me too, to let me live as I want." Meg said. "I hadn't thought of it that way," Len said.

"I think my father would rather I had fallen in love with Griff than you." Meg announced.

"This is true," Griff said, "It would have been all the simpler if you would have fallen for me instead of an angel.

"You know as I think on it my father has given me away enough. I think I will give myself away at the wedding."

"A capital idea," said Aunt Ruth.

*****

"I think we should get married between the realms." "The space between your cottage and Griff's." Len said.

"I can't think of anywhere else except a park to be so open."

"Meg, darling you are forgetting Griff is about the only demon going to be present most will be angels."

"I only want to weed out the faint of heart." Meg said smartly.

"You being the bride my dear will do that on its own." Len returned. "Oh how you want to turn me into an angel."

"Because you act more angel than demon." Len added for good measure, "You seem as though you have a good soul."

"I have you fooled."

"Never."

"Where is Storm?"

"Napping."

"I'd like to nap with you."

"I'm sure nothing would make you happier, Len, but not until after the wedding. Everyone will excuse us Storm but a second one on the way so soon would be unforgiveable."

"How far is the wedding again?" "A week away."

"Then we are free to play?"

"As free as I allow. I still want some space between my children." "I thought you only wanted one."

"I wanted none. But with you I know there will be more than one."

"I'm glad we agree on that."

"Kind of hard not to," Meg said with a grimace. "It isn't that bad."

"Then you be the one to give birth. I'll be the one to smile and made to feel great for doing nothing big."

"I'll be your total slave." "You already are."

Len shrugged, "I guess you are right."

*****

The week went by in a flurry of activity. Meg was secretive about her dress. Although she proclaimed it wouldn't be tradition white or older traditional red. The red about sent Aunt Ruth into a faint. That would be a total disrespect to an angel wedding. Meg knew that but she also knew she would be true to herself.

Meg wouldn't pretend to be something she was not. And she was far from a naïve innocent. She was pretty worldly herself. She would have to be if she was older than the first few colonies. She had been raised by an Indian woman. Though there had been those that thought the infant that washed up on the beach was cursed.

So, she had grown as an outcast in her adopted family as well. It was only after the whites came to the continent that the demons started becoming bolder. They liked the freedom and disrespect they had of the earth. It was easier to deceive them than the Indians that had tricksters and looked out for such folk.

Griff came around when she was hanging around younger demons. Once they found out she knew nothing of her father she would became the outcast. But Griff had been different. He didn't care if she knew her father or not. He had helped guide her through trials and tribulations. Only disappearing when he needed to work for his master.

Meg should have suspected something. A demon doesn't do anything out of the kindness of heart. And yet that is what it had appeared Griff had been doing. She hadn't questioned his motives once he joked about marrying her. Well, she had thought it was a joke but it hadn't been. He had always been serious about marrying her. It would have been a prize to marry his lord's daughter. It would make him a master of all.

Meg had never really felt that way about Griff. He felt more like an older brother. Especially when he had helped her build the cottage. It, of course, was built with demon magic so where it was could be built over by humans and they would never know. Though her cottage remained untouched.

*****

Len wondered what Meg was thinking and doing with her time. He was already getting pretty possessive. He didn't want her around Griff by himself. Which had made Meg laugh. Len just couldn't help himself, he trusted Meg but he didn't trust Griff.

Len wanted to make sure the wedding happened as scheduled. It was something that he had been waiting for since before he had met Meg. He'd loved her at first sight. She hadn't changed a bit. That was the demon in her. He knew that and yet he still loved her.

Perhaps because Meg acted more like an angelic soul than she did a demon. It also helped that she looked human. Len thought it was the mortals in their DNA that had fallen for one another. At least that is what he wanted to believe.

Aunt Ruth was a good sounding board but she tried to not interfere too much in their affairs. Meg seemed to enjoy feeling around to see what was in her good sense and what was beyond. She had brought up wearing a gold dress. Aunt Ruth had calmly said no to that. Meg had wisely backed down. She didn't want to fall out of Aunt Ruth's good graces.

*****

The lane between cottages was sparkling with flowers and ribbons.

Meg walked slowly down the lane. Her thoughts on all that had happened in the past year and a half. Never did she think she would know who her father was. Though she did have to refer to him as he who would not be named.

She glided by in a dress of silver. It was a compromise since white represented innocence and she was far from innocent. She would have opted for pink but it would have looked odd on her red hued skin. The color glimmered in the sunlight. Meg was loud as a bride.

As Len had predicted only one demon showed up on Meg's side. Griff was stoically there. On the other side Ruth held a protesting Storm. He didn't understand all this adult stuff and didn't want to sit still. There were other angels she didn't know. Luckily, Len's father hadn't shown up. She might have hurt him.

Time slowed down as she got closer to the arch where Len and she would share their vows. She got there and still was awed by the number of angels to attend her wedding. As those numbers would influence the next of her children's orientation. She smiled at such a wayward thought. It would certainly be disapproved of.

Finally she made it to the arch. "I give myself to this man."

"Very good," said the mortal priest. He went into the normal sermon. "I, Fallen Taylor Angelou, take you Meglatonlori Airagotti to be my wedded wife. To love and to cherish from this day forth until the end of days."

"And I, Meglatonlori.Airagotti, take you, Fallen Taylor Angelou to be my wedded husband. To love and to cherish from this forth until the end of days."

"I now pronounce you husband and wife. You may kiss your bride."

Len took Meg in a fancy dip for the kiss. They both put spirit in the kiss which Griff heckled being the only demon there. Meg blushed becomingly even though it was difficult to tell with her skin tone. Only those that knew her could see the change in color.

The reception as part of the compromise was at the angel apartments. Though Griff complained of the candy smell he went to the reception. There the angels felt free to party and a few female angels even danced with Griff. They were of course trying to convert him to their side.

Meg laughed as did Len at the futility of it all. Griff was a confirmed demon. Though there were a couple angels he kept paying attention to. He was charming but, he should have known no one was going to sleep with him. He left the reception in a funk.

The joy filled couple did not bother saying anything. They were busy dancing with different angels. Meg was having the time of her life. Though she would never admit it to her husband some of the angel men lusted after her and she was getting a good dose off of them. To their credit they were younger half breeds. They weren't full blooded angels. That would have taken the blush off the sinless rose he thought angels to be.

She hoped the night wouldn't end. That way she could continue to have fun with the angels. But soon enough instead of going to the cottage, Len took her to his apartment, Aunt Ruth being kind enough to keep Storm over night.

*****

Meg woke first. Len tried fooling around some more but Meg was having none of it. She went up to Aunt Ruth's apartment and got her son. She was no longer feeling the vibe of being around all the angels. Len knew she had held back on some of her kinkiness because of being in the land of angels so he was ready to return to the cottage.

All was taken care of but Len's father. He could still come out of the woodwork with some demon to try to steal Storm. Because Art really was that stupid. Griff agreed with Meg which of course annoyed Len.

"But I bound him."

"A demon binding by an angel. Not as good a magic as you would expect," Griff explained.

"Then why let me do it to begin with?"

"To let you feel you are protecting your son." Griff said.

"We can't kill him."

"No, he is immortal." Griff agreed.

"What would you have us do?" Len asked.

"You are not bound by demon law call your father here so that I may bind him."

"Are you crazy?" Meg called.

Griff tucked her chin, "It is the only , Megawatt. I have to bind him to a master. He is after all answering to no one.

"Are you saying?" Meg started.

"I wish I could bind him to he who is not named."

"Doesn't that mean he will work for him." "Exactly," said Griff. "He'll be a cutthroat master."

"Does it matter to you, M? Are you already so kind hearted you care for your enemy?" Griff taunted.

"I say forget about him, but Len where are you on this?"

Len looked to his wife and then at Griff, "I love my son more than anything. I don't want there to be jeopardy to any of my children so I agree to this demon deal."

"You can't take this back, Len, and we are talking about your father." "A father that is more demon than Griff. My mother didn't raise me because she killed herself after I was born. Because of the sin of having me. That is why Ruth raised me."

"What?!" Meg protested, "I thought we were done with secrets." "That is the last one," Len said with passion.

Meg shook her head. It was difficult to fault Len for that one. She had never asked why Aunt Ruth was the one to raise him. She had certainly had time to ask.

"So are we going to do this now?"

Griff nodded, "Now or never. Remember to use his full first name so I have more power over him to bind him."

"I call to you Arthenius. I call to you Arthenius. I call to you Arthenius."

Arthenius appeared to them all, "What in the name of Hades do you kids want?"

"Funny you should ask." Griff said snidely, "I want to bind you Arthenius to he who would not be named." "Quit playing." Art said.

"I want to bind you Arthenius to he who would not be named."

"Don't. I don't know who this is but stop it."

"I bind you Arthenius to my master he who would not be named." Both Griff and Arthenius disappeared.

Meg hugged Len, "You did the right thing. It was the hard thing but it was the right thing."

"I had to protect our son." "You mean our children."

Len looked at Meg, "You don't mean you are pr—"

"Not yet but I see it in our future."

"I see it in our future too."

Thank you

Thank you for reading my first published work. I hope you enjoyed Rules for Dating a Demon: The Get. If you did please consider leaving a review on Amazon or Goodreads. Reviews make or break a book and I would appreciate all the help I can get.

Book 2

If you liked Rules for Dating a Demon I am coming out with Book 2. Losing Faith in October. *

In the war between heaven and hell there exists angels and demons. Faith is an angel that is hopelessly attracted to the forbidden fruit of demon Griff. Will the angels win or will they be Losing Faith.

Due to health issues Losing Faith is due out Summer 2020.

Rules for Dating A Demon 2

Losing Faith

By AMANDA HUMES

Losing Faith: Chapter 1

"One thousand nine hundred and ninety-seven." Griff groaned as he pushed up again. He worked out almost every day. It was work to maintain his tight 12 pack. That he allowed to be shown off in a shirtless state. And he had thick muscular thighs revealed by cutoff black jeans.

Faith watched from a distance, in the secret demon forest in New York. A forest in a void that is not well known to any other than demons and a few angels, between two cottages that Griff had built. It rivaled the majesty of Central Park.

Faith was attempting to not let the drool fall from her lips. Currently she was double damned. She was first lusting, and then to top it off, the object of her lust was a demon overlord. However, much she tried to hide it; it was the naked truth. She would endure the stigma of fallen if it could be for this muscular hunk of a demon.

Angels paled to his red skinned glamour. Even the most fit of angels seemed like little weaklings. Of course, an angel was not supposed to be so superficial. Faith did not know where her lust came from but she gloried in it. She could watch Griff for the rest of eternity. With a pout to her lips she turned away from the demon of her fantasies.

It was time to get back to the angel apartments. A middle-sized building that housed angels and select part angels. She stifled a cringe at the thought of being with so many angels and in a place so white. A few years ago, she had felt ill at ease with the rest of the angels. Faith had known there was something different about her. More than her subtle gut and lopsided grin had deviated from the norm.

Len was also overweight, a voice reminded her. She pushed the voice away. Len was a male. Males were not as scrutinized as females. Also, Len had found love, in a gorgeous demoness, no less. Leah, the school headmistress had not really spoken of it; however, Faith knew he was the one that had been assigned to be her mate. They were to be the perfect pair. The Fallen angel and the flawed one.

She was jealous of the welcome, however reluctantly given that Meg had. Of course, Meg was a demon different from most. She had a heart, though she may still be soulless. That soullessness had come in handy when Len's father had tried to spirit their son, Storm, away. It allowed Meg to combust into flames when angry.

Faith wanted to be the beautiful one. She craved the attention and adoration. Faith knew she was not cut out to be the angel that she was.

Though she lacked the courage to say anything. She went through the motions. What motions there were. One would think of Victorian England.

Leah, the instructor, nudged Faith as she bent another needle during needle work class, "This is sewing class, not jewelry making, Faith." Making the small white room feel even smaller.

Faith bit back her retort. Angels were too pure to wear jewelry, especially handmade stuff unless it had holy meaning. She tossed the offending metal into the scrap bin. It made a clang against the rest she had lining the basket.

Leah lifted her brow and Faith frowned in contrition. She hadn't meant to make the noise, but that was the main attention she got. Sometimes she felt like she was trapped in a sitcom and not in a good way. Maybe she was the angel incarnation of Lucy. That was how much trouble she got in.

Next was scripture reading class. Leah looked pointedly at Faith to begin. Again, Faith shrank. Her reading voice was terrible. She struggled with the words as though she were beginning a foreign language. After one mangled verse she was given a reprieve.

Leah went on to another reader. Faith crumpled even more into herself as she heard the words spun into a near musical verse. All the other girls smiled and cooed. Nobody mangled the verses, not even one stutter was heard the rest of the day.

When the rest of the girls were dismissed Leah held Faith back, "I know you are trying but surely you can reach in a bit deeper and find the inner angel." Faith held back her tears. She would not let Auntie Leah reduce her to tears. Not now, not ever was Faith's solemn vow to herself.

Faith went up to her small apartment. It was fit for a nun how tiny it felt. White unadorned walls before her, with a small white cot and tiny white desk. It was a cage for her wandering soul. She was just happy that it was not on the sixth floor. She had a fear of the number six. That number was unlucky for her and, of course, part of the number of the beast. Did that not beat all she was in lust with a demon overlord and afraid of the beast of end times?

Of course, not all demons were good looking. Some were monstrous half human, half animal combination. That was certainly not the case with Griff. Faith fanned herself still feeling flushed with pure lust. But too afraid to summon him.

Oh, to have the courage to summon him. If only she knew his full name, she would have power over him. Yes, a reference three times would summon but the closer to the full name the more power the summoner held, and less tricky a demon could be.

That is why the curse was Holy Lu and not his full name and not said regularly. No one wanted to disturb the king of that dominion. It almost paralleled saying the Lord's name in vain at least to angel ears and eyes.

Faith crushed her eyes shut. Nothing about her was natural. An angel should not be thinking of a demon even when he is in his incubus mode.

They were to resist the carnal cravings that linked angels to their human side. Now a human was supposed to cave into the carnal demands.

The tears that she had vowed not to expose leaked out. Probably because of the force she used to crush her eyes. Faith felt her shame.

*****

Griff was not stupid, nor was his sense of smell deadened. As he did his sit-ups he knew an angel was watching him. That candy smell was sickeningly sweet. Even being around Len did not make him immune to it. Griff just wondered who was watching him. If only it were a high-ranking angel that was attempting to convert him. He was suave enough that he could make the switch. That would earn him more favor with his demon lord.

He had lost some street credit by "letting" Meg fall in love with Len. Griff had hoped for the lovely Meg to fall for him. Then he would have been nearly a king of the underworld. He gritted his teeth in frustration of all he felt he had lost. In the battle between heaven and hell the angels had won a strong one. It was only fair if one of their fair angels fell to the charm of a demon.

Instead of looking at her he let her get her eye full and slink away.

His would be more than a sloppy seduction. Next time he would turn to her and reveal he knew she was watching him. He decided to have a meeting with one of his under lords, instead. Jebediah was a loyal follower. He was a under lord that had a few get, children of demon blood, under his belt. They were grown and under lords of their own rank and file.

Jebediah was a handsome demon and if the Griff was of the type to indulge with men, he would have had him when he was a sweet young thing. Griff was after all an incubus, an attractive sex demon. But he was of the procreative mode. He wanted his own string of get. Of course, being as old as he was, Griff already had had many get. All without the angelic mode of marriage or the bonding of demons. There had been many demonesses that had wanted to be tied to him. But he always slid free. Of course, he had mainly thought of Meg as worth bonding with. If he was going to sink to linking himself to one person, it was going to be a step up. That was his promise to himself. That is if he indulged in being monogamous. So far, he had not the inclination to be tied to one. Just because he felt that way did not mean he could not help a glamourous angel fall.

Jebediah knelt before Griff. Jebediah was easily mistaken for his son.

Griff signaled for Jebediah to get up. Jebediah maintained about an eight pack. He was shorter than Griff. But had the same red skin and inky black hair and human faces. Though Jebediah had a gap between his front teeth whereas Griff had perfectly straight teeth though a little rough in the face. "Evening, Master Griff."

"Evening, Jeb."

"You did not call for social reasons, did you?"

"Hades, no!" Griff disclaimed, "I called you to let you know to be on the look-out for my shadow. I have an angel trailing me."

"A rogue angel?"

"If I am lucky a lovely soon to be rogue angel."

"Sounds delightful. It seems like centuries since we turned an angel."

Griff thought on it for more than a minute, "It quite possibly has been." He would not admit to his underling he had been pining over an unacknowledged get. A high bred unacknowledged get was unheard of. Though, that was what Meg was. Griff could not betray his master by letting his underling know that Meg was the daughter of their master.

Griff cursed the heart of his master for it allowing himself to be tricked into not acknowledging such a beautiful and powerful daughter that Meg was. Griff was entrusted with her care and made sure she lived a somewhat carefree life. As much as her cursed status would allow. An unacknowledged get was lower than a mortal's bastard because demons were usually braggards and would claim all children.

Jebediah only knew Griff was around Meg but just thought he was taken with her. She was known for not only her unacknowledged state, but also how impossible she was to get into bed. After all, Griff, was known to love a challenge. Meg was certainly a grand challenge.

Jebediah liked a challenging woman too. But unlike his master he believed he knew when to quit. Jebediah loved willing women. There were too many in the city to give it up for one that cannot be had. Because contrary to her nature Meg was monogamous to Len.

Just because he was a demon did not mean Jebediah was against monogamy. He just could not see being attached to one being. That was one thing about Jebediah, he was pan sexual, though he was more attracted to the females. Jebediah decided since he was in New York there was only one place to go, Angelique's.

The bar was one of the favorites of the city. It was the place to be mortal and demon alike. It was smoky and dark. The smoke helped squash the smell of fire and brimstone demons had. The hostess was a very engaging blonde demoness with light skin. Her blood lines might not be the purest of demon's but she had certainly converted many a mortal to the dark side. Her true name was not Angelique though if you said it three times it would pull her to the caller. She would tease and let people call her Angel or A.

Jebediah went to the bar where Angelique held court though there happened to be more than one bar. The establishment was a towering five floors. High rolling demons held court on the top two floors. It was rumored that the top two floors where made of gold and had high rollers. Jebediah at times went to the second floor where there were the poor man's gaming tables. Occasionally, he took a conquest up to the third floor where there were beds and again, poor man's entertainments of strippers. Jebediah was denied entrance to those top floors because of his low rank. Some days he spent his time on the second floor where there was always a good game of Poker. Angelique gave him a wink as he drank his usual. Some would call it boring, but he had a rum and coke. He decided he was going to get drunk as he could. Tomorrow was soon enough to follow Griff to catch the angel watching him.

COMING TO KINDLE OCTOBER 4TH, 2019. *
https://www.amazon.com/Rules-Dating-Demon-Losing-Faith-ebook/dp/B07V5FL7M3/ref=sr_1_4?   keywords=rules+-for+dating+a+demon&qid=1563029379&s=ga 4

Due to health issues Losing Faith is projected to be published Summer 2020.

FOR MORE RULES INTERACTION

I have started a fan group for Rules For Dating a Demon on Facebook. It is called Rules Fans:
https://www.facebook.com/groups/2065713987058523/

Special Thanks

I would like to thank the late Rod Sterling for his Twilight Zone. My history and English Professors for encouraging my mind with the myths both Roman and Greek.

About the Author

Amanda Humes was born the last of seven children in a blended family. Her mom lovingly calls all the children the Brady Bunch plus one.

She graduated from Southeastern Community College, where she was a paid tutor, in 2000 on the Dean's List with an Associate Arts Degree. (College was fully paid for by scholarships and grant money.) While in school, she did paint, and had two or three paintings in art a local show. One painting was the school magazine, although credit was featured in accidentally given to another artist.

Amanda stayed home, in Keokuk Iowa, to help her parents. In part because her dad lost his job in 2000. She has had a few jobs, from selling fireworks, worked in a bindery (a factory that cut greeting cards, made folders and other junk mail.) Unfortunately, the bindery went out of business in early 2001. Eventually, landing in the shipping department of the home office of Dadant and Sons Inc. There she packed and shipped packages (mostly to foreign countries) and answered beekeeping sales calls and questions for nearly seven years.

Amanda currently works at her local Walmart as a Cashier and does occasionally work as a service desk associate. She has worked there since 2008. (She did work in layaway when it first came back where her shipping department skills came in handy.)

In 2014, she went back to school. She wrote Rules for Dating a Demon in 2015 as part of a class project for American Public University. She graduated Honor Role class of 2016 with a Bachelors of Arts in English. With encouragement from her oldest sister, Lori, she is currently writing Rules For Dating a Demon 2: Losing Faith.

When not working or writing, Amanda enjoys reading, drawing, dancing to music, and she, even, started jewelry making. When not working on Saturdays she enjoys day long road trips around the Tri-State area of Iowa, Missouri and Illinois.

www.ingramcontent.com/pod-product-compliance
Lightning Source LLC
Chambersburg PA
CBHW020120310726
48970CB00002B/720